Other Sean Michael Novels

Amnesia
Between Friends
Bite
Bus Stories and Other Tales
The Broken Road
Caged
Catching a Second Wind
Chosen
Don't Ask, Don't Tell
Fine as Frog Hair
Making a Splash: A Going for the Gold Novel
Need
On the Sand
Out of the Closet
Perfect Ten: A Going for the Gold Novel
Personal Best I-III: Going for the Gold Novels
Personal Leave
A Private Hunger
Second Sight
Secrets, Skin and Leather
Tempering
Three Day Passes
Tripwire
The Velvet Glove Vol. I & II
Where Flows the Water
Windbrothers

Other Julia Talbot Novels

Historical Obsessions
Jumping Into Things
Landing On Both Feet
Manners and Means
Perfect
Taking a Leap
Tomb of the God King

Other BA Tortuga Novels

Hurricane
Hyacinth Club
Latigo
Living in Fast Forward
Long Black Cadillac
The Long Road Home
Old Town New
Racing the Moon
Rain and Whiskey
Redemption's Ride
Sara's Cowboy
Steam and Sunshine
Stress Relief
Timeless Hunger
Tropical Depression

This is a work of fiction. Names, characters, places, and incidents either are the product of the author's imagination or are used fictitiously. Any resemblance to actual events, locales, organizations, or persons, living or dead, is entirely coincidental and beyond the intent of either the author or the publisher.

Mates
BAREBACK ANGELS
For Life Copyright © 2007 BA Tortuga
Fur and Phobia Copyright © 2007 Julia Talbot
Running with the Wolf Copyright © 2007 Sean Michael
An imprint of Torquere Press Publishers
PO Box 2545
Round Rock, TX 78680
Cover illustration by Skylar Sinclair
Published with permission
ISBN: 978-1-60370-285-0, 1-60370-285-7
www.torquerepress.com

First Torquere Press Printing: February 2008
Printed in the USA

Mates

Torquere Press, Inc.
romance for the rest of us
www.torquerepress.com

Mates

Table of Contents

Foreword - 7
Fur and Phobia by Julia Talbot - 9
Running with the Wolf by Sean Michael - 75
For Life by BA Tortuga - 159
Contributors - 241

Mates

Foreword

The politics of a wolfpack have fascinated humans for centuries, almost as long as the intricacies between men and women have baffled us.

Combine them in one volume, and you have a powerful combination.

Mates features all the intensity that we've come to love from werewolf stories; primal urges, pack struggles, hot loving. There's much more, though, because these mates aren't couples. There are three people to account for in each tale, three sets of emotions, three points of view. New relationships and old, new werewolves and wolves that were born that way; all of these factors make for conflict, for romance and for danger.

The stories in Mates are compelling, loving, and full of all the things that make werewolves so fascinating.

We hope you enjoy them as much as we did.

Torquere Press

Mates

Fur and Phobia
Julia Talbot

Deb searched through her Rolodex, looking for a particular number, her long, painted nails clacking on the plastic as she flipped. The cards were all neat, organized, little labels pasted on the cards. It wasn't an issue of organization, really. It was an issue of memory.

Under A for 'Aaron'?

W for 'Weiler'?

T for 'Trainer'?

M for 'Man's Best'...

Bingo!

She grinned, plucked the car out and dialed, pencil tapping impatiently on her desk as the phone rang. And rang. And rang.

"Oh, for the love of... Oh! Aaron, darling! It's Dr. Ballard. How are you, dear?"

"Hey, Doc." Deb could hear dogs barking in the background as Aaron answered, the phone clunking against something and Aaron grunting. "How's it hanging, lady?"

She chuckled, pushing her curls off her shoulder.

"Oh, dearest. Life is delicious, as always. It sounds wonderfully busy for you. The kennel full?" She did adore Aaron, from top to bottom. Such an interesting man, so good with dumb animals.

"Uh-huh. And the living room, the backyard and the run..." A low chuckle came across the line, masculine and happy. "So what can I do for you, Doc?"

"I have a client, lovely. A sweet, smart lady with a bit of a problem that I think you're the perfect cure for."

"Yeah? Darn it, Mop, you big hairy freak. Get down. Sorry. What sort of a problem?"

Deb tugged Abby's file over, flipped it open. "She's a horticulturist. Researches plants. Quite clever at it, too. Just finished grad. school. Unfortunately, she has an unreasonable cynophobia that's preventing her from doing her job."

"Well, that's not good. Lots of dogs out in people's yards." He laughed again, and she could hear the crunch of large teeth on a bone. "There, you monstrous beast. I can take the referral, sure. How do you want me to play it? Tough love or slow introduction?"

"Mmm..." Now there was a fun question. "I can see benefits to either method. She's not a shrinking violet, but she's definitely a girl."

"Well, Doc, you're the shrink. I don't want to damage her psyche forever doing it the wrong way."

"Now, now. Are you suggesting you might do it the wrong way?" She chuckled, chewing on the end of her pen. "I'd start easy, darling. Let her relax. You can always be hard after."

That got a bark of laughter that had her grinning right along. Really, he had the best disposition. "Okay. Set it up for me to meet her somewhere else to begin with, then. Lunch, or something."

"How about Fellini's? They've got a little of everything. How does tomorrow sound? Say noon-ish?"

"That sounds fine. I'll leave Lee in charge of the kennel. Thanks for the job, Doc."

"Anytime, darling. Stop by sometime for coffee. We'll chat."

Well, she'd ogle. He could chat.

"You got it, Deb. Oh, by the way, tell your cousin that she can pick up the poodle anytime. He doesn't chew his fur out anymore."

Sweet, sweet boy.

"Thank you, honey. I'll let Abby know. Oh! Her name's Abigail Mann. Blonde, green eyes, sweet little thing - she'll be looking for you."

A low growl came through, but not an unhappy one. "Oh. That sounds nice. I'll be looking for her too. See you, Doc."

"Goodbye, darling. Enjoy her and do keep me informed."

She chuckled to herself as she hung up the phone. That was, after all, the very best part.

Being informed.

***

"Lee! Got a referral from Deb. You're gonna have to watch the place for a bit!" Aaron unwrapped Woofer from the umbrella stand, trying to get the big sheepdog to work on a leash.

Lee walked out of the kennel area, wiping his hands on a big rag, smile lines crinkling around his green eyes. "You look happy about it, lover. Is she pretty?"

His long-time partner knew him too damned well. "Deb says she's all girl. She's got fuzzy-phobia."

"Well, that could be inconvenient at a certain

time of the month, baby."

***

If she could, Abby would just beat herself.

Honestly.

Four years as an undergrad. Three years in grad school. The perfect internship. The job offer of a lifetime and the first client she goes to see? The first yard she goes into to take samples?

She ended up in the back of an ambulance, hyperventilating, shaking so bad she couldn't stand.

It was stupid. Everybody loved dogs.

Everybody.

People bought calendars of the awful things, even.

She rolled her eyes, tightened her ponytail and pushed the restaurant doors open. Well, Dr. Ballard said this man was the finest dog trainer in the state, that he'd helped tons of people overcome their phobias.

That he could help her keep her job.

Damn it.

The place smelled like garlic and fresh baked bread, and had that sort of careless ambiance a restaurant only got when they stopped trying. The hostess smiled at her and grabbed a menu. "I bet you're meeting Aaron," the perky brunette said, pausing dramatically.

"You do? I mean, I am, but how did you know?" What? Did she have 'Scared of Dogs. Need Help" tattooed on her forehead?

That cute little nose wrinkled right up and the girl whapped her arm with the menu. "Well, he said he was meeting a pretty little blonde. Come on, he's back here."

Oh, great. Surely that's not how Dr. Ballard described her. She didn't want to come off as a ding-bat. She wasn't one. She just had issues. An issue. A very specific dog-related issue.

She made sure there wasn't any potting medium on her hands, that her nails weren't filthy as they headed toward the back, where the scent of garlic and butter was even stronger.

The hostess led her to a table for two, occupied by a guy with curly brown hair, tanned skin, and a smile that just beamed when he stood to meet her.

"Hi. Abby? I'm Aaron Weiler."

"Hello Mr. Weiler. It's nice to meet you." She held one hand out to shake, managing a real smile in response. Oh, he wasn't hard on the eyes. At all. "Thank you for agreeing to meet with me."

"No problem at all. I'm always willing to lend a hand to one of Deb's." He actually came around to pull out her chair, his shoulder brushing hers. His aftershave smelled nice. Kind of outdoorsy.

She got settled in, brushed a leaf off her jeans. "Dr. Ballard's a huge help. She. I. I mean, I assume she told you..."

"Yeah. She really only sends me phobias." He sat too, nudged her menu over. "What do you say we just chat a little first?"

"Okay. Sure." God. She was a 'phobia'. Weird. She opened her menu, looking over the different meals, none of them really making an impact. "Do you know what's good here?"

"The special today is a seafood manicotti. It's in-tense. Or they have a great capellini pomodoro." His hands were large and square, scarred, with clipped, clean nails. She noticed them as her eyes wandered.

"Intense as in spicy?" The scars were fascinat-ing, really. Nothing like she'd ever seen before.

"More like flavorful. It's got plenty of spice, but man, it's just like an explosion. Pancetta. Shrimp.

This garlic parmesan marinara..." He grinned, teeth flashing again. Wow. He had bright brown eyes...

"It sounds good." The way he was describing it, it sounded like sex. Like really good sex.

"It is." He looked at her as he laid his menu down. "So Deb says you're a landscaper?

"Not really. My specialty is insect hardy plants. Keeping plants healthy without a bunch of chemicals to ruin the water table." She shrugged, smiled. "It's less boring than it sounds."

"Hey, that doesn't sound boring at all. So you're actually more like a botanist? I'm all for clean water. Iced tea, please," Aaron told the waitress, smiling at the girl and getting a wiggle and a giggle. He was good looking enough, sure, but not stunning. There just seemed to be something about him.

"Water with lemon, please." Her best friend, Annie, would call it animal attraction. Of course, Annie's specialty was primate communication and the woman saw animals and attraction in everything.

"Are you folks ready to order?" The waitress stood poised, pen hovering over her pad, smiling at Aaron.

Aaron looked at her. "I want the special, but if you need a few more minutes?"

"No. No, the manicotti sounds good. I'll have that." If nothing else, she could eat half and take half home for dinner.

"Great." He waited for the waitress to leave before plopping his elbows on the table and leaning forward. "So I guess you get a lot of curious mutts wanting to say hi."

Curious. Right. Hungry, maybe. Toothy, definitely. "Yeah. I. People don't keep them in as well as they ought sometimes."

"Oh, sometimes they just get out, too. Dogs can be pretty clever and boisterous. So. Did you have a bad experience as a kid?" He looked so earnest.

"Not that I can remember, really. I know that I can't. I mean, I never have been able to do the 'aw, cute, puppy' thing. Maybe when I was little bitty?" She didn't know, it didn't make any sense.

"Okay. Oh, garlic bread." The basket hardly hit the table before Aaron scooped up a piece, dipping it in the marinara that came with it. "Oh..."

He closed his eyes and sorta...hummed.

Man, if he did everything like he ate, somebody was a really, really lucky girl.

"It's good?" She stole a bite, nibbling. Mmm. Garlic. Butter.

It had that little bit of crunch, but was soft on the inside. Yum.

"Yeah," Aaron said. "It's good. It's the little things in life, yeah?"

"Yes. Yes, I think so." She nodded, nibbling another bite. "So do you breed dogs?"

Maybe that was where the scars came from.

"I do. I also have a kennel for pay, and another for training. I do a lot of obedience work. Behavior modification, you know?" His eyes twinkled as he smiled at her. Yeah, behavior modification.

"Do... Do you get bitten a lot?" At least she wouldn't hurt him back. The worst she did was pass out.

"No, not really. Oh, the puppies have sharp teeth, but they don't mean anything. The one thing you need to remember about dogs? They're generally desperate to please you. Really."

"Have you seen Cujo?" Not that she had, but the DVD cover had given her nightmares for a week.

"Oh, come on, only Stephen King can make a Saint Bernard a horror villain. They're bred to save lives." Their salads came and Aaron waved his fork as he talked. Thankfully it was still empty.

Of course, the image of bib lettuce and romaine flinging across the table made her smile, made the hard little ache in her belly ease. Maybe she could do this. Maybe.

"That's much better. You have a great smile." Well, that look was as warm as the one the garlic bread had gotten. "So tell me what you hope to accomplish."

"I just don't want to lose my job." She met those pretty eyes, dead serious. "I can't pass out every time a dog comes into a yard, you know? Ambulances are expensive and the sirens embarrass the college administration."

"Okay. I like that you're pretty level headed about it. Some folks expect me to magically make all of their fears go away. Some do end up loving and owning dogs. Some, though, are lucky to learn to be able to look from a distance."

The pasta came, and damn. It smelled great.

"I just want to stay conscious and functional." Abby unwrapped her fork, put her napkin in her lap. "Not necessarily in that order."

"I bet we can do that. I assume you'd rather not just jump right in and come to the kennel."

Her hand started to shake and he reached out to hold her wrist. "I'm sorry. That was classless."

"I'm sorry. I know it's stupid. I know." God, why couldn't Dr. Ballard have found someone old, ugly? Someone that it didn't matter if she came off as the world's biggest idiot?

"No. It's not stupid. I totally get it. I'm scared to death to fly. And unless you have a fear like that it's hard to understand. We'll go slow. How do you feel about me bringing a dog with me the next time we meet? She can stay on one side of a yard, we can stay on the other. It'll be a good first step."

Those big brown eyes were so full of understanding.

Hopefully it would be a little dog. A little trained dog. "Okay. Okay. I'll try."

She could do this. She *could*.

"Good. Now, take a drink of water and try the manicotti. You'll love it. I promise."

He did put her at ease. He really did.

Maybe this wouldn't be so bad after all.

Though it really couldn't be better than the pasta. Because damn. It was really, really good.

***

"So, she couldn't do it, huh?" Lee asked, sautéing garlic and shallots in a pan.

"Nope. I've met with her four times since she called to cancel that one meet, and she just hasn't even been able to deal with the dog hair on my pants. Bless her heart, she has a bad case."

"Is she pretty?" Marinated steaks slid into the pan, the sizzle telling him the pan would be just hot enough to put a crust on them, to make them rare.

"Glorious. Blonde hair, green eyes. Curvy."

"Awoo. She sounds nice."

"She is. Damn it."

They'd had supper. They'd flirted, had some warm touches; a hand at the waist, fingers trailing over the skin above an elbow. He'd just never managed to get her to meet a dog. Or to let him come to her house.

"She'll fall to your charms, lover. Then I get to meet her, right?" One dark eyebrow went up, Lee giving him a bright grin.

"You do. I share, you know that. I love you best."

Lee pulled the pan off the heat, covering the steaks with foil to let them rest before coming to put an arm around Aaron's waist.

"I know you do, lover. Feel free to show me."

Aaron took a kiss, his cock starting to take an interest in the proceedings. "Anytime, baby. Anytime."

***

"I just don't know if I can do it, Deb," Abby murmured, barely audible over the clack of her assistant's keyboard out front.

"Is it just that you don't trust him, darling?" Deb twirled her pen, staring at the way the faux tortoise shell caught the light.

"No! Oh, no, I think he's wonderful. He's really helped me out when we meet dogs out on the street. Really. I just don't think I can deliberately put myself in the situation."

"Have you tried?"

"I told him I would, but then I backed out."

Deb could hear the tears in Abby's voice. The self-defeat.

"Well, you'll have to try again. Call him. Tell him you want to meet him again, this time with a dog. A small one. What is it I always say?"

"That it's better to face your fears in a controlled environment than to be blindsided by them."

"Exactly. Call him, darling. You won't regret it."

"Oh, you never know. I have untapped depths of stupidity where he's concerned."

"Hmm?" What on earth did that mean?

"Nothing. Okay. I'll call him."

"Good girl. See you on Tuesday, lovey."

"I'll be there."

Deb hung up, staring at the phone for a moment before shaking her head. Such an intelligent girl. So messed up about dogs, which would keep Abby and Aaron from striking up a real relationship.

Such a shame.

*****

He brought Muffin. The tiny Bichon was so friendly, so happy, and had that round headed sweet look that almost anyone could love. Aaron also brought Lee, who stood across the little green area of the park and held Muffin's leash.

Aaron met Abby on the other side of the park. Bless her heart, he was afraid she'd keel over otherwise, the way her hands had shaken when he'd mentioned Saint Bernards or wolfhounds. God knew what she'd do when faced by a mastiff.

There. She stood with her hands in her back pockets, looking around a little nervously. Grinning, Aaron made his way over. He'd bet she had no idea that doing that made her breasts push out at that angle.

"Hi, there," he said, smiling.

"Hey. Hey. How're you?" Her hair was pulled back into a loose ponytail and the scent of soil and growth all around her.

"Good." He was, too. The sun shone bright. The grass had that fresh cut smell. Man, he had the worst urge to play Frisbee. "How're you?"

"Nervous. Still full from the barbeque we had for dinner a few nights back.."

"That brisket stays with you, huh? God, I love that." Bouncing a little, Aaron took her elbow, really lightly, so she didn't feel like he was forcing her. "Okay. Over there," he pointed, "is a very small dog. We're going to move closer, stopping when you start to feel uncomfortable, so I can gauge your reaction, okay?"

"Okay. Is it friendly?" He could feel her, trembling in his hand.

"It is." Oh. Man. Poor Abby. Aaron really felt for her. "Tell me when you have to stop, okay? Let me tell you about Muffin. She's nearly ten, really cute, a little lazy, not at all yippy."

"Muffin? And is ten old for a dog?" Her eyes were fastened on Muffin, watching every motion.

"It is. If you figure the old one human year is seven dog years thing? Yeah. She's like, seventy." Muffin was putting on an acute show of cute, romping around at Lee's feet.

"She... she's very active, for an old dog. Is she yours?" Her steps were slowing.

With his free hand, Aaron gave Lee the signal to have Muffin sit. She did at Lee's command, looking adoringly up at the handler. "No, she's Lee's now. The man with her. She belonged to an elderly lady who went to a nursing home. The family didn't want her."

"No? Wh...why? Does she bite?" Abby slowed down further, almost stopping.

"No." Lord. Aaron moved his thumb, caressing her elbow, soothing her. He hoped. "No, she's a doll. They said she shed too much. They left her in a box at the shelter, with this nasty-ass note."

"They... they got rid of her because of her hair?"

That was better. She wasn't shaking now. Sympathy was good. "Yep. She'd been with her owner eight years. Then boom. Out."

"That's sort of mean." Abby leaned against him a little, still watching Muffin. "Does she... I mean, are they smart enough to know?"

"You mean does she miss her mom?" Aaron sighed, feeling just as bad for Muffin as he did for Abby. "She looks for her every day."

"Oh." Oh, those pretty eyes filled with tears.

"After two whole years?"

"Yep. She likes Lee a lot, though, see?" He motioned again and Lee bent and opened an arm to Muffin, who wiggled right up to lick his face and settle so he could carry her.

Abby winced, took a step back. "He could get his face bitten, his eyes."

Damn. Aaron stepped back with her, his hand settling on the small of her back. "They have trust. Look how big he is next to her. She knows he could do her a lot more damage, right?"

She nodded, curves pushing right into his hand. "Yeah. Yeah, he doesn't look worried. She... well, she sort of looks like a cotton ball. With eyes and teeth."

"And a pink tongue." Yeah. She kinda did, and Abby didn't, and Aaron tried not to get distracted by the feel of her. "Can we try a few more feet?"

"Okay." She stepped closer, one step, two, then the shivers started again. "I bet she gets dirty."

"I bet you do too." He tried finding the common ground. "You probably dig more than she does."

That got him a laugh, that ponytail just swinging as she grinned. "I would imagine so. I bet I'm easier to clean."

"Oh. Uh-huh." Down boy. Any further flirting could wait until Muffin was gone. Aaron cleared his throat. "Yeah. She, uh. She likes baths. Do you?"

"I love the water. I swim every day. What about you?"

"I'm a big fan. I love to go to the lake. Splash around." They moved up two more steps.

"Yeah? Me too. Pools. Hot tubs. Lakes. When it comes to the water, I'm easy." They were almost right there, Abby looking up at him, eyes focused.

"Yeah? You like bubbles?" She'd look fantastic in a bubble bath, suds just to her nipples...

Her cheeks went bright pink and he'd bet Abby wasn't thinking about Muffin anymore. "I do. I should buy stock in peach bubbles. I soak every day, if I can."

"Peach, huh?" He grinned, tried not to sniff too obviously. Damn, he liked the smell of her. He really did. Stroking her back, Aaron stopped them, not wanting to shock her with how close she was. "I like that sort of pine scent, myself. Not like Pine-sol, but like...I dunno. Forest."

"Pine oil is very distinctive. Masculine. Sexual." Muffin got tired of waiting, barking and bouncing, trying to get his attention. Abby's eyes went wide and she pushed right behind him, hands on his hips.

"Sorry. I. Oh, sorry." Making himself solid, Aaron backed her off a few steps. "I think that's enough for today. Can you go over there and wait? I owe Muffin a treat and some petting. Then I can maybe take you for coffee?"

"Coffee. Okay. Coffee. She's a pretty color. You can tell her, if it matters." Abby took off like a bat out of hell, moving across the grass.

Shaking his head, Aaron went to give muffin pats and biscuits. "Good girl. She thinks you're pretty. Yes she does."

Muffin wagged and panted, little button eyes just shining, watching Abby go.

"I know, honey. You wanted to say hi. Next time." Her ears perked as he scratched behind them. "Thanks, babe. She did well."

Lee chuckled, nodded. "Looked like you were doing pretty damned good yourself."

"I was. I hope to. You know me, honey." Aaron winked. "Best go get her before she bolts. Here, have a five. Get Muffin here a cheeseburger on the way home."

"I will. She is pretty. You know you're going to

have to share, right? Oh, and don't forget, it's first waxing, tonight. Be home before dark, lover."

"I told you I would, but we'll have to cross that one when we come to it. Right now she's afraid of Muffin. Can you imagine what she'll think of your hairy butt? I'll be home before dark." Clapping Lee on the back, Aaron gave Muffin one last scratch and headed off to corral his coffee date.

She did have a pretty ass, nice and curvy, enough to make a man howl. She was sitting on the tailgate of a wee green Japanese pickup, feet swinging, eyes just a little shiny. "I'm sorry. I tried not to freak. Honest."

"You did really well, hon. We just got a little... well. I got distracted." Winking, he sat next to her, nudging her. "So. You like lattes?"

"Yeah. You?" There was a sprinkling of freckles right on the tip of her nose. Cute.

"I'm all for it. And cake. I love cake." He had a horrible sweet tooth. Thank goodness the dogs kept him so active, or he'd have a paunch. "Let's go. I'll even let you drive."

"Oh, you're a modern man." He got another chuckle, Abby wiping her eyes. "Okay. Come on. Topaz's has cheesecake with real strawberries."

"Yeah." Aaron watched the gentle sway of her ass as she got in the driver's side, and he licked his lips. Maybe they could get that cake to go.

***

Abby got to the coffee shop without one squealing turn, no shaking hands, nothing.

She even made jokes, got the CD into the player without dropping it, laughed. Go her.

"So, are you a black, strong coffee guy or a latte guy?" See her. See her make conversation. Go her.

"Oh, I like both," Aaron said, hand on the small of her back as he guided her to the counter. "But today I think I want a nice plain cappuccino so nothing overpowers the strawberry cheesecake."

"I love the hazelnut lattes - not too sweet, not too strong." God, his hand was warm, solid. Strong.

"They're good. I like peppermint, though, too. In the winter. Makes my nose tingle." He laughed a little, the sound warm, intimate, really shaking off the freak outs from the little dog.

"Ooh. I love candy canes to stir my coffee. It seems so decadent." They ordered - a latte and a piece of cherry pie for her and a cappuccino and cheesecake for him.

"Oh. Or cinnamon sticks in apple cider." His eyes sparkled, and she'd swear he bounced a little. He was so enthusiastic. Made her wonder where else he would work so hard.

"Oh, now you're making me wish it was December and snowing." She paid for their food, grinning back and up at him.

"Snow is fun. Do you ski?" Oh. Was that a leading statement or what? Like he might want to be around come ski season? Down girl.

"I try. I'm not great at it, but I enjoy it. I love the fire-buttered rum-cuddling under a blanket afterwards part." Okay, desperate much?

She turned to apologize when the shop door opened, a couple coming in with a giant beast who was tugging and yanking at a too-tiny leash. Oh. Oh.

"Abby? What..." He trailed off as he turned too, stepping in front of her. "It's okay, honey. He's not coming at you. Okay? We'll get you on out of here."

Aaron waited until the dog went toward the "order here" area before pushing her to one side and taking her arm, pulling her around in a wide arc toward the door.

"D...d...dogs don't belong in coffee shops." Especially not big dogs with huge teeth and tiny leashes. *Especially* not them.

"Oh, it looked to me like he was a regular. There. We're out. Come on and sit down. Or do you want me to drive you home?"

"I." Her cheeks burned, eyes fastened onto the ground. God, she was pathetic. Pathetic.

She just wanted to go home and hide until, oh, next year.

"You shouldn't let your cheesecake go to waste. I'll take you back to your car after." And then drown herself in her bathtub.

"We'll go to your place, then. No worries, honey, okay?" He was being very sweet. Somehow that made it worse. They went to her car, Aaron gently prying her hands off her pie box and drink cup.

No crying.

None.

Just get in, drive. No crying.

"Here. Let me, okay? I know you can drive, but you don't have to." Yes. Okay. She went dutifully to sit in the passenger seat and Aaron started up her car, nudging her to put her seatbelt on before handing her the food.

"I live over on the hill. Green Street." She wasn't crying. Or sniffling. Or anything.

"Okay. We'll be there in a few." He drove so smoothly, no jolts or sharp turns, just easing around, asking for directions when he needed to turn. "Okay. Here we are."

"Thank you. I'm sorry. Come in. You can at least drink your coffee in peace." Her house was little, neat, old. Simple. The neatest thing about it was the English garden in the back, the rose bushes in the front.

That and the claw-foot tub where she was going to spend the rest of her evening, anyway.

"Thanks. You did really well, you know." He took everything from her and let her go open the door.

"Yeah. Gloriously. I'm a fucking basket case who can't even buy coffee without embarrassing herself."

"No." They got inside and Aaron set everything down, turning to put his hands on her shoulders, his eyes dark and serious, his voice firm. "No. You had just dealt with your fears in a controlled environment and then got blindsided. You did fine. I'm pleased."

"If you keep being nice to me, you'll make me cry." God, he had the prettiest eyes.

"We can't have that." Laughing, he got her coffee. "Here, drink up. The sugar and caffeine should help."

"I'll go get some silverware. Find a seat." Her house still looked like late grad school garage sale, but she had a real sofa and one good end table that her dad had refinished.

"Thanks." He waited for her, took his fork, but as she just sat and stared at the table he put his hand over hers. "Look, maybe we should put this in the fridge, have it later. Is there something you do to relax?"

"Like yoga? No. I soak in the tub, go swimming." She turned her hand over, touching him. "I'm sorry, Aaron. I... Man, I wish Dr. Ballard had found me an ugly old scary guy to see me as a nutjob. It's hard to come off as classy and attractive when you're wigged."

That had him laughing right out loud, squeezing her fingers. "Oh, honey. You're wonderful. I'm glad we got to meet. And I look forward to more work with you. Is it selfish to hope you don't get over your fear too quick so you need me longer?"

His touch made little tingles run up her arm.

"Probably." She couldn't help smiling, rolling her eyes just a little at herself. "I'm not always a dork, you know. Sometimes I'm quite clever and fun."

"I bet you are. If you're this neat when you're terrified..." Goodness he was a charmer. His fingers slid up to close around her wrist, rubbing over her pulse-point.

She hummed, fingers curling right along with her toes. "You're warm, like a furnace."

A really, really studly furnace.

"I always run a little warmer than the average guy. Only my nose gets cold in the winter." Aaron grinned, scooting his chair around a bit. "So is it nosy to ask for a tour?"

"Oh, no. No. Come on." She did laundry last night, so no random dirty unmentionables scattered anywhere. "I just moved. I'm renting, but the landlord says I can buy, if I want."

"Yeah? It's nice. Does it have a yard?" Following along, Aaron stayed close to her, occasionally brushing against her.

"Oh, yes. It *does*." She grinned, maybe bounced a little as she led him through the still-empty dining room and into the tiny, bright kitchen. She'd painted the walls yellow, the cabinets white and the bar-stools bright blue. She loved it. "My father helped me install the French door so I can look out onto my garden."

She opened the door, let the intricate garden with its paths and hedges, its flowers and tiny pools and trellises, speak for itself.

"Wow. That's a heck of a garden." She could

swear he sniffed. Hard.

"Thanks. It's looking good. I want to plant some lemon trees in pots, I think, so I can drag them inside in the winter." She inhaled, chin lifting. It did smell good -- green, alive, spicy.

He actually ventured out, touching this plant, admiring that one, turning in circles almost like he was chasing his tail. "This is amazing. Really."

Abby just beamed, doing a little wandering herself, finally in her element. She plucked a leaf here, a weed there, just making sure everything was growing, happy.

She shrieked a little as he came back in a rush, grabbing her and dancing her about in a little foxtrot or two-step or something. "I really like your garden."

Abby laughed, her hair coming loose from its band as they danced around, falling around her face. "Thank you. It's sort of my passion."

"You can tell. It tells me a lot about you." They gradually slowed, standing together, arms looped around each other's waist. Aaron just sort of... stared right into her eyes.

Oh.

She didn't think too much. There were times it was just a pointless waste and staring into those chocolate brown eyes was one of them. Abby took a step closer, face lifting for a kiss.

She got it, Aaron bending to press his lips against hers, soft and easy. His tongue traced her mouth, pushing inside gently, opening her. Tasting her.

It was so easy, to just relax and open up, let her tongue slide against his. As the kiss deepened, she pushed closer, rubbing into Aaron's warmth, arms wrapping around Aaron's neck.

He made a soft sound, hand flattening at the small of her back to hold her close, his tongue pushing in again and again to taste her. Oh, he was good at that, that kissing thing.

Her fingers slid into Aaron's hair -- Oh, soft. Soft and thick, lucky man.

"Mmm." His arm slid more fully around her, sort of bending her back over bone and muscle, arching her hips right into him, against his thigh. "Pretty, honey. Real pretty."

Flatterer. She smiled against his lips, belly tightening up as she stretched. Mmm. Coffee.

He must have felt her smile, because he chuckled, turning them, lifting her a little so she rubbed against his hip, just like that. Man, he was strong.

Heat flooded her, little jolts of lightning firing between her nipples and clit, making her moan, making her hips tilt just so. Okay. Yeah. That was. Uhn.

"Like that. Yes." His voice became a throaty growl, his teeth nipping at her lower lip, but not hard enough to hurt. Just enough to make her tingle. Holding her up with one arm, Aaron put his other hand over her left breast, pushing, squeezing, his palm right over her nipple.

Oh, that felt perfect. She pushed right back, moaning as his fingers got a little tighter, the sensations got a little sharper. "Aaron. You. It feels good."

Better than good.

"Uh-huh." Tasting her again, Aaron moved them, carrying her, finding a flat surface. A wall? Her wicker lounge? Something. Aaron eased her down, his weight heavy and good on her.

One of her legs wrapped right around Aaron's hip, tugging them together even tighter. Oh. Oh, he was hard. Hot. Wanting her.

His heat pressed against her center, even through their clothes, his cock sliding hard against her, pushing at her clit. It made her head fall back, made her clutch him and moan.

His lips found her neck and she shuddered, tingles slamming through her. Her toes curled tight, chin lifting so he could kiss more, lick, taste.

Again, he gave her exactly what she wanted, lips sliding down her throat, his tongue pushing at the spot where her pulse beat hard. He hummed, sucking lightly, not hard enough to mark, but enough to feel.

The sounds that came out of her were embarrassing, so wanton and needy, but he didn't seem to mind them, hips shifting faster and harder against her.

"Abby. You're making me crazy." His words came just as hot as her sounds, breathy, dark, little puffs of air against her skin. He rocked them, pulling her leg up higher on his thigh, opening her.

"Is... is that bad?" God, she was wet, wanting more, wanting to feel Aaron hot inside her.

"No. S'good. Very good." Oh, so was his mouth on her breast, even through her shirt and bra. Aaron was so hot he practically burned her.

"Good." She tugged at his shirt, wanting to touch skin, to feel that heat from the source.

Leaving her for half a moment, Aaron knelt up and pulled the shirt off over his head, his smooth skin, just lightly fuzzed from nipple to nipple and then down all available to her, ready. Amazing.

"Oh, yum." Her fingers slid all the way up, hips rocking a little faster at the sensation of heat and skin and hair on her hands.

"Oh, it's only fair to share." He grinned, white teeth flashing, and stopped her when she would have pulled him down again. Instead he tugged at her shirt. "You too."

"You showed me yours, I show you mine?" She

chuckled at his grin, worked the t-shirt out of her waistband, hoping to God she didn't have on a scary bra with big holes in it. Oh. Cool. Lace. Excellent.

"Mmm. Nice. But this has to go too." Easily lifting her, Aaron smoothed off her shirt, undid her bra, baring her to his hot gaze. "Oh. Look at that."

He didn't even hesitate, just bent and licked at one nipple, getting it good and wet.

Oh. Oh, wow. The difference between hot tongue and cool wind just made her nipple draw up into a tight bud, almost aching with the pleasure. "Aaron. I. Oh."

"Yes." Lips closing around her, Aaron sucked strongly, tongue flicking back and forth. His hands stayed busy, counting her ribs, the bumps of her spine.

Her hands wrapped around his head, held on and kept that amazing, hungry mouth right there, right where she needed it. Oh, fuck. She could come, just from that tongue and the friction of Aaron's body.

He rubbed and licked and sucked until she was just crazy with it, her whole body arching and rolling. His cock throbbed against her, still separated by their clothes.

"I want. Aaron, please. More." She shoved her hand down between them, palm pressed hard against Aaron's shaft, fingers curling around his balls.

That got her a grunt, a wide-eyed look, his face turning up from her chest so he could stare at her. "I...I don't have anything, Abby. I want you, but I wasn't. I didn't."

"I do. Inside." She should anyway. There should be a couple left from Jack. "Come... come see my bedroom?"

"Yeah. Okay." There was no way she could feel self conscious with him smiling at her like that, hoisting himself up to grab her and sweep her inside. Aaron just made her feel at ease, period.

She was cuddled right against his side, one hand on the small of his back. It was easy, to lead him into her little room, the windows filled with plants, the double bed still mussed from this morning. She walked over to the nightstand, trying to feel sophisticated and mature, pulling out her tiny stash of condoms and setting them on the headboard.

"Oh. Perfect." His hands slid around from her back to cover her belly. They felt huge on her, covering her. Then his fingers started in on her jeans.

Abby leaned back, arms reaching up to play with his hair. It was easy to suck in a little, make it easy for him to unfasten the button, slide the denim over her hips.

Aaron pulled them down, his cheek rubbing her belly as he bent to pull her shoes off too.

"Mmm. You smell good, honey."

Her cheeks heated, everything in her just melting. Her hips shifted, almost rolling of their own accord, the skin of her belly sliding against his face.

He nuzzled, his chin rubbing her curls. He pressed a kiss just below her navel, hot and wet.

"You make my knees weak." Husky, rough -- her voice sounded like it belonged to someone else.

"Good. You don't make me weak, I have to admit. Make me hard." His thumb rubbed down, spreading her, glancing off her clit.

"Oh!" She jerked, lips parting as she went up on her toes, legs just shaking. "Oh."

"Come on, honey. Lie down. I want to, too." Aaron slid right back up her body, muscles surging as he stood and swung her around to push her back on the bed.

The box springs squeaked as she bounced, legs sprawling a little as she cuddled into the mass of comforters. "You're wearing too many clothes."

"I know." Man, he could have a mischievous smile. He really could. She'd bet he was into everything as a kid. This was no kid, though, who took his jeans off, popping the button, the zipper making a long, scratching noise.

She didn't moan, but she couldn't stop her tongue from sliding over her lips, her eyes following the motion of his hand.

The glory trail so lived up to its promise. When he shoved his pants down and kicked his shoes off she got a fine view of a muscled belly, firm thighs, and a hard, hard prick.

It was the easiest thing on earth, to roll over onto her belly, reach out and let her fingers slip-slide down his belly to that heavy cock. Smooth and stiff, like silk stretched over steel -- it made her mouth water, made her pussy throb.

"Uhn." His whole body jerked, all those lean muscles rippling for her as he moved close, almost like she'd pulled on him.

Mmm... That got him close enough to... Oh, yes. Her tongue slipped all the way up his length, tracing the ridge where the head flared.

"Oh, God almighty." His cock twitched violently before Aaron pulled away and crawled up on the bed with her, pushing her back, kissing her breathless.

Skin on skin was just what she needed, legs twining with his, fingers tangling in his hair. Oh, he was strong, wide, covering her.

She could feel him now, like she hadn't been able too when they'd been separated by cloth, hot, little drops of moisture sliding against her hip. He rocked, kissing her, nibbling her lips like she was a treat, even as he reached for the condoms she'd dropped.

He smelled good, too. Not soapy or cologne-y, just rich and male. On her sheets. Arousing.

"You wanna put it on me?" Aaron wagged the

condom between them. Laughing, his eyes just dancing. She couldn't believe that was cute, but it was.

"You just want to be touched." Abby giggled, grabbed the condom and worked it open.

"Hell, yes. Want to touch you, too. Want to be in you more." Aaron wiggled, proving how hot he was for her, poking at her that way.

"Be still now." She ducked her head, rubbing her cheek against his chest as she grabbed his cock, slid the latex on him, smoothed it down with both hands.

"Oh, easier said than done, honey." His muscles quivered with the effort, she could see it, could feel it on her skin as he arched up against her. The hair on his belly was much softer than the stuff on his chest, springier than the hair on his head. The contrast fascinated her.

Her lips found one of his little nipples as her fingers slipped down to cup his balls, rolling them, weighing them.

"God!" He didn't pull away, didn't shrink from the touch. In fact, he pushed into it, humming, clutching at her. Oh, it was good, they way he responded.

He had the most amazing hands, huge and hot, dragging over her skin and tugging her closer.

"Now, honey. Yeah?" Aaron moved, pulling her legs apart, tilting her hips up, but waiting, his thick cock poised at her entrance.

"Now." She arched up, letting him in, groaning as he stretched her, filled her up.

His forehead rested against hers as he surged into her, filling her to the hilt, hips pressing hers. A harsh groan echoed against her lips, his voice raw in his throat.

"Abby."

"Uh-huh. Good. It's good." She moaned against his lips, fingers digging into his shoulders. Such pretty eyes. God.

They started moving, touching, their skin rubbing along every inch of the other's bodies. He filled her so good, stretched her, pushing in and out, the friction almost unbearable.

The hair on his chest teased her nipples, while the press of his cock made her arch, hips rocking demanding that Aaron move faster, harder. He gave her just what she needed, his low sounds almost animalistic, his skin slapping against hers.

It was primal, amazing, hot, and it went on and on. Aaron's eyes blazed down at her, almost glowing, and she was captured by their color. She reached up to touch his cheek, the spring wound tighter and tighter inside her until she thought she might explode.

Aaron pushed into her over and over, bracing himself on one arm so he could touch her with the other hand. His fingers rasped against her nipples, slid over her belly, finally settling where they joined. Tiny movements made her gasp, made her buck, and he kissed her as he pressed hard at her clit, tongue pushing deep.

Abby came, squeezing down on Aaron's cock, crying out as she flew, her whole body wracked with shudders and covered in goose bumps.

"Oh... Abby." She could feel him moving inside her, feel it when he shot for her. It was hot and sweaty and he shook for her, and if she wasn't as relaxed as she'd ever been in her life, she might have been a little smug.

"Mmm." Stretching under him, Abby stroked Aaron's back, smiling at the ceiling. Wow.

"Wow," Aaron said, echoing her thoughts, lips sliding against her jaw.

"Can you stay?" Her fingers curled in his hair, and she watched it spring back into place when she let go.

"Hmm?" He propped up to look at her, and the weirdest expression crossed his face. "What day is it?"

"Um. Saturday."

"No, no, the day if the month."

"The fifteenth." She thought. It was kind of hard to remember with him inside her, on top of her.

"Shit!" Aaron scrambled up, sliding out of her and tossing the condom aside. "I'm sorry, Abby. I can't stay right now. In fact, I have to go. I... Oh, God. I'm sorry."

Bending to kiss her hard, he smiled, stroking her hair. Then he gathered up her clothes and just... left. Which would have been bad enough, with the whole fuck and run thing, but it was even worse.

He'd left without even having a car to drive home.

***

"Abby, darling, I'm sure you're just overreacting." Deb twirled in her chair, one foot waving in the air, her pump hanging on just her toes. Those shoes were going into the rubbish as soon as she got home.

"He just left, Deb. Ran away. I mean, I admit, I took far longer than the appointment should have, but I'm... I'm just not sure I can meet with him again. It seemed really unprofessional."

"Oh, dear. Shall I call him for you?"

She could hear Abby shifting, probably nervously moving from foot to foot. "Would you? He didn't leave me a number, and I just want to make sure I didn't offend him somehow."

"Of course you didn't. I'll give him a ring-a-ling." And a piece of her mind. Really, Aaron was usually so charming, so polite.

"Thanks, Deb. I'll see you on Tuesday, right?"

"I'll be waiting with bells on."

Abby hung up and Deb pulled out her Rolodex. She'd be waiting with bells on, and with Aaron Weiler's head on a platter.

Young people these days could be so rude. No matter how pretty they were.

***

Aaron woke up with Lee, curled up with his head on Lee's belly. They'd gone to sleep nose to tail, fuzzy as could be, locked securely in their little basement hideaway. Now they were kinda nose to more interesting parts of the human anatomy.

Nuzzling, Aaron breathed deep, smiling at the scent of musk and male.

Male… Female. Oh, shit, he needed to call Abby. Apologize.

"Hey, lover, where are you going in such a hurry?" Lee caught him by the leg, reeling him back in to grin down at him. Those light brown eyes were lit up with mischief, and there was a definite morning hard-on pressed against his hip.

"My coffee date. I left in a hurry yesterday."

"A man might get jealous, Aaron."

"Bullshit. You know I love you more than my luggage. Did we get Gil to come in and do the feeding this morning?"

"Yeah. Some of us were concentrating on business."

Oh, asshole. Aaron turned and bit Lee hard on the shoulder. "You'll like her. If I can get her to talk to me again."

"You will. You have those big puppy dog eyes." Lee moved closer. "I could smell her on you when you came home."

"Mmm. You liked?"

"I did." Lee's mouth slid wetly across his shoulder, tongue flicking out to taste his skin. "She smelled good. You smelled like sex. I would have eaten you alive if we'd had time."

Laughing, Aaron rolled, straddling his Lee and bending to take a lip-mashing kiss. "You can now."

"I can!" Pinching his ass, Lee licked his lips, kissing him again, starting to rub up on him.

"I can wait—oh, there. I can wait to call."

"Right here?" Lee's hand found his cock, stroking up and down, giving him the best kind of friction.

"Uh-huh. Christ, Lee. More." His own hands started to wander, rubbing down Lee's back, clutching at that muscled ass. Goddamn, Lee had a tight, tiny heiny. He did love it. Aaron pushed at Lee's crease with his fingers, needing to feel. He didn't feel guilty; he and Lee played a lot. He did feel the need to reconnect.

Moaning, twisting, Lee gave it up, spreading for him. His fingers slid against that hot little hole, so different from Abby's slick center, so ready for him anyway.

"Love how hot you are, baby."

"Shut up and get inside me, lover."

"Oh, yeah." Scrambling, he grabbed the lube. He got his fingers slick, pushing two into Lee's body, stretching that tight hole. Aaron didn't need a condom. Lee and him, they couldn't give anything to each other.

He couldn't wait until Abby knew that...

"Stop thinking about your girl and get your butt over here." A sharp edge was starting to enter Lee's voice, a growl of need.

"Maybe you just need to make sure I'm not thinking of anyone else."

Lee stared at him over one shoulder, teeth bared, ass pushing back on his fingers. "Now."

"Yeah." Oh, God, look at that man. So good to him. So hot. Aaron gave Lee what he needed, fingers pulling free so he could replace them with his cock, the heat from Lee's body making him moan. Making him sweat.

"Love you, baby," he said, draping himself over Lee's back.

"Uh-huh. Keep going." Lee's voice was all wolf, now. All fur and teeth and primal instinct.

Aaron went with it, slamming hard into that beautiful, muscular body, his own sounds reduced to grunts and snarls. He bit at Lee's shoulder, needing to taste male musk and salt, reveling in the differences between his encounter with Abby and this hard mating.

If he ever got them together, he might just explode.

Lee arched for him, reaching back to grab the hand Aaron used to hold his hip, pulling it forward to touch Lee's cock. His fingers wrapped around the shaft, his fingertips tracing the heavy vein beneath. The smell of them together made his mouth water, made him want things they didn't have time for right now. So instead he bit down on the nape of Lee's neck, stroking hard and fast at the beautiful prick in his hand, daring Lee not to come.

His lover spent for him, wet heat coating his hand, and Aaron moaned, lips on the back of Lee's shoulder, pressing hard while he pumped his release into Lee's body. So good. Like home. Necessary.

Chuckling, Lee slumped down on their bed, taking him down too. "So, when are you going to tell her?"

"About you? Or about the whole fuzzy thing?"

"Either. Both."

"I just met her, Lee. Hell, I probably pissed her off running like that. Give me time."

Lee patted his butt, laughing. "That's one thing we have plenty of, lover."

"Mmmhmm." Aaron snuggled in again, putting his head on Lee's shoulder. He needed to call Abby, but he wouldn't be able to see her until the moon cycled out of full, anyway.

It could wait.

***

The phone rang not five minutes before Abby was leaving for her appointment with Deb.

Abby bit her lip, staring at it. What if it was Deb, calling to cancel. Abby had held it together pretty darned well, really, considering the incident she'd had Monday. It had involved a bloodhound, an aloe plant and a panic attack.

She really felt like she needed some therapy.

Finally, she reached for the phone, clearing her throat. "Hello?"

"Abby! I'm so glad I finally caught you. I've been trying to call and apologize for days now." The warm voice went right to her toes, even though the little voice in her head was telling her toes to stuff it.

"Okay, you've apologized. Thanks for all of your help, Aaron. Now,--"

"No. No, don't hang up, Abby. I want to make it up to you."

"How? You know, you left without even a car to drive home in. I didn't think I was all that, but I never thought I was chew my arm off ugly."

"You're not! It's hard to explain, but I'd like to try. Over dinner."

Dinner. With Aaron. The prospect thrilled her as much as it gave her the heebie jeebies.

"I'm not sure that's such a good idea." She peered at the clock. "I have to go see Deb. Bye, Aaron."

She hung up, feeling a little vindicated, feeling like she'd run out on him this time. Maybe, just maybe, if he called again, she'd say yes.

***

Aaron waited outside Deb's office, holding tight to the leash, It had taken a hell of a lot to get the damned guard to let him in with an animal, even when his canine companion showed all the signs of being a service dog.

A service dog. Lee was gonna bite his ass off.

Still, Lee would be the best thing for Abby to get over her fuzzy phobia. He was a man in wolf's clothing, after all.

Of course, if she stayed in there with Deb much longer, he was gonna have to take Lee out to tinkle on the perfectly manicured grass.

Lee leaned down, chewed on the cuff of his jeans. Asshole.

He didn't kick Lee in the teeth, though. The secretary would stop smiling at him.

Of course, then Lee bit his ankle. Damn. That stung.

"Aaron. Darling." Deb came sauntering back, eyes dancing. "You did come. How sweet."

"I told you I would when you called to cuss me out." He grinned and stood, kissing her powdery cheek. "Is it as bad as all that?"

"No, of course not, you charming little shit. She's in there, doing breathing exercises."

"Oh. Bless her heart. I could go in and see her if you'll hold Baby, here." He handed over Lee's leash, knowing he'd give Deb hell.

"Baby. How adorable. Is he housetrained?" Oh, god.

"Yeah. You have to watch the marking behavior, though. He's the jealous type." Time to escape. Aaron handed her the leash and headed in to see Abby.

She was sitting cross-legged in a chair, eyes closed, breathing deep and slow.

Aaron picked another chair and sat, waiting for her to notice him. He didn't want to interrupt her meditation.

Her eyes opened and she just stared over. "Hey. How's it going?"

"I'm good. How are you?" He smiled. staring into her pretty eyes.

"Okay. Had a rough week, but it's getting better."

"I'm sorry if I made it worse." He really was. Aaron hated that he'd run out on her like that.

"It's okay. I'm over it." She fluttered one hand a little, tried to smile.

"Well, you're doing better than I am, then." He squatted on his heels in front of her, taking her hands in his. "I want to apologize. I'm sorry."

"It's cool. I..." Her lips twisted. "I just..." Her voice dropped to a whisper. "I thought it was good.

"It was, honey. I told you I've been trying to call." Bringing her hands up, he kissed them, letting his lips linger.

She made the sweetest little noise, just humming for him. "Your lips are warm..."

"Your hands are cold, honey." Man, something besides him had to have happened.

"Yeah. It's been a bad week. She pushed up her shirt, a series of pokes and scratches there. "I had a run-in with a big dog. She didn't hurt me, but the aloe did."

"Oh." Aaron bent to kiss each mark. "We need to get back with the program."

"I tried. It was so big and barking."

"I know. I bet." He leaned a little closer, letting his warmth seep into her. "I brought a beautiful animal with me today, if you want to try again."

"Is it scary?" She leaned right back, cuddling a little. That's right, honey, come here.

"Well, I don't think so. He's a lover. Very gentle. He's big, though. Can you trust me?" She had no reason to, really, but he hoped she would.

"I'll try." She met his eyes, trying to be so brave.

"You're a stud, honey." Standing, he drew her to her feet, knowing Lee would charm her socks off, even all furry.

She shuffled to the door with him, fingers twined with his. "I feel like a weinie."

"You're not. You're a very brave lady, and you absolutely don't have to worry about Baby." He held her hand, thumb stroking her skin.

She hummed a little, the sound soft, scared, and sexy, all at once.

Aaron could smell her fear, though, so he took it slow. Easy. He put his body in front of hers. Of course, when he came out, Deb was on the little sofa in the waiting room with Lee half in her lap, tongue lolling as she scratched his ears.

Lee barked once, tail wagging and Abby peeped, stepping back.

"Oh. Oh, he's big."

"He's a sweetheart." He held out his free hand and Lee came right up, slow and sure, rubbing against his palm.

Lee chuffed happily, tongue lolling. Those bright

eyes shone up at Abby, just pretty as all get out.

"He's a handsome one," She said, clinging to his hand like there was no tomorrow.

"He is. And very well trained." Pushing his luck, for sure, but Lee would never do anything to scare Abby. He knew that.

Lee licked his fingers, then sat back on his haunches, smiling at them.

"There. See? All he needs is for you to pet him." Grinning, he urged her to reach out with the hand holding his.

Her hand shook violently, but she managed, fingers dragging over Lee's fur.

Lee made a happy noise, leaning gently into her touch. Oh, he knew it. Knew Lee would like her scent, her look, just as much as he did.

Lee nosed her palm and she squeaked again, almost pulling away.

"No, no. He's just saying hi, honey. See?" Stroking Lee's ears with his other hand, he hummed, subvocalizing a little.

Panting, pushing close, that tail just wagged and wagged. Deb stood up, nodded happily.

"Very good. Very, very good, Abby."

Lee gave them a doggie smile, tongue pushing out to lick Abby's hand again. So sweet.

"He... he won't bite me, right? I don't want him to bite me." He couldn't tell if she was crying or laughing. Maybe both, a little.

"No. No, he's not a biter." Not unless you asked him to, and hell, she wouldn't. At least not yet.

Lee leaned back, one paw lifted up to shake with her, dear and sweet as can be.

"Oh, look at that." Deb clapped her hands, laughing delightedly.

Abby, bless her heart, bent a little, shook Lee's hand.

Nuzzling her politely, Lee stepped back, giving her room.

"See, honey? No harm, no foul." Score one for the fuzzy team.

"He's pretty. What's his name?"

"I call him Baby." It wasn't a lie. Not one bit.

"Oh. Cool. N...nice Baby. God, I feel stupid."

Lee chuffed, eyes just dancing. Little shit.

"He likes to be petted. A lot. Maybe you could give him a treat. Just to see that he won't hurt you." Aaron pulled a little bag of spicy Cheetos out of his pocket.

"I don't... I don't know if I can." She leaned hard against the door frame and he tossed Lee a Cheeto, the quick fucker catching it easily.

"Watch." He handed Deb a snack. "Gentle, Baby."

Lee sidled over, slinky anything, wanting it. She tossed the treat and Lee grabbed it, chomping away.

"See? He's a gentle giant. Why don't you try?"

Ally's eyes were filled with tears, but she took the Cheetos, breaking the first one, dropping the second and then actually tossing the third.

Patiently, Lee worked a little closer to her until he was sitting almost on top of her feet. He actually got to lick her fingers.

She didn't cry; she didn't freak out. Hell, once she actually laughed. This might be a fucking win.

Aaron sure as hell hoped so. How was she going to handle it when he and Lee changed otherwise? Lord, what a mess.

Abby leaned against him a little bit, almost re-laxed. "He's so good. Not mean at all."

"Most animals aren't mean, honey. They're just exuberant, or scared of you, or curious."

"Yeah. I guess. I just... They surprise me and

poof. Passed out."

"Well, we'll have to work on not being blind-sided by them. Maybe you should come out to my place this week. Thursday will be a slow day. I don't have a lot of kennel booked then, and no appointments for training."

That way he could get her on his territory, get her to meet Lee as a man.

"I could. Yeah. Yeah. I. I will." Look at that stubborn chin.

"Good. Good. Thank you, honey." They could leave her with Deb now that she trusted him again, now that she would see them again.

"You're welcome. I... I'm going to sit down for a little bit."

"Okay, hon. I have to go, okay? Let you have some time with the Doc, and take Baby on home. Will you answer when I call?" He kissed her cheek.

"I'll seriously consider it, yeah."

"I hope you will." Aaron gave her a look just for her, intimate, he hoped hot. He needed to see her again. Needed to let Lee charm her as a man.

Her cheeks went hot and, damn. Damn, he could smell her; Lee had to be going nuts.

Time to get out and get Lee home before things started poking out and making with the embarrassment.

Deb patted his arm. "You did very well, darling."

"Thanks, Lady. Does this put me back in your Rolodex?" he murmured, moving Lee toward the door.

"You know it. Good boy. Very good boy."

"Thanks." He stroked Lee's ears. "Come on, Baby. Let's go home."

Lee leaned in hard, rubbing against him, tail thumping against his legs.

They headed out, Lee pretending to heel like a very good boy, at least until they got outside. Then it was jerk Aaron all over the place to sniff at stranger's crotches.

Ah, the punishment phase had started. Lee tugged and danced, spinning him around and chuffing at him.

Sighing, he let Lee play for awhile, knowing if he didn't he'd hear no end of it at home. Then he pulled Lee to the Jeep. "Baby, I want to take you home and do bad things to you. Will you behave?"

Lee sat.

Stared up.

Wagged.

"Come on." Grinning, he opened the door, letting Lee hop up, scrubbing at those long ears before starting up and heading home.

Lee muttered and barked, just talking to him, telling him how much he liked Abby, how hungry he was. Dork.

"I told you. I knew you'd like her. And yeah, she's soft. Really curvy." That had made Lee drool. He just knew it. Lee nosed right under his jaw, tongue flicking at his skin. "Mmm. Stop it, baby. You really want me to get pulled over for crimes of a furry kind?"

That soft chuff of laughter tickled his neck, then Lee sat back.

The drive home took forever, and it took him even longer to get the door unlocked and get all of the mutts squared away. Finally, Aaron turned to find a naked Lee, human and waiting and ready. Hallelujah.

"Hey." Lee stepped up, lips sliding on his jaw. "You owe me a reward."

"You think?" Aaron turned his head the tiniest bit, letting his lips meet Lee's, happy as fuck to have him back in the human flesh. So hot and smooth. Naked, where he still had his scratchy clothes on.

The laughter that pushed into his mouth had him grinning, had Lee rubbing and hard against his thigh.

"I guess next time I have to be the guide dog, huh?" He wrapped his arms around Lee's waist, hands on that fine, muscled ass.

"Yep. You can wag and sit pretty. You're so fucking good at it."

"I do try." He wagged a little, rubbing against Lee, his cock rising in his jeans.

"Mmmhmm. I'm a fan of trying..." Lee caught his bottom lip, tugged a little. "You bringing the pretty lady to play?"

"I'm gonna try. I think she'll like you even better like this, huh?" He sure did. Kissing his way along Lee's jaw, Aaron hummed, savoring salt and musk."

She'd better. I'm way less toothy." The words were punctuated with a bite.

"Still bitey, though." Uhn. God, he loved it when Lee got a little growly.

"You can take the fur out of the human..." He got another bite, and another.

"Uh-huh. But you can't take the fuzzy out of the man." Aaron let one hand drag around to the front of Lee's body, fingers trailing along the strip of fuzz that lead down to the base of that sweet cock.

Lee bucked up, face raised to him, lips open. "Uh-huh. More. Now, Aaron."

"Hungry baby. I love it when you're wanting." His touched the underside of Lee's prick, the soft sacs beneath.

Lee spread for him, eyes wide and shining for him.

"So damned hot, baby." Those heavy balls

pressed against his palm, and Aaron rolled them, played with them a little, just jonesing on it. Hard, strong hands landed on his shoulders, Lee rocking, rolling with it, teeth bared.

"One of has too many clothes on." His free hand grabbed Lee's wrist, pulling up to put Lee's clever fingers on his shirt buttons.

"You think?" Pop. Pop. Pop. Damn, Lee was good at that, if fucking hard on the threads. His shirt came down off his shoulders, Lee reaching for his belt.

"I think. Wait. I'm not sure I can think with you doing that." He grabbed that sweet cock and jacked, pulling gently at first, then harder.

"Who gives a fuck about thinking?" Lee's fingers went all clumsy and rough, focus shattering as he did his touching.

"That's it, baby. Just like that." He loved it when Lee was wild for him. Loved the snarl in that deep voice.

The room spun a little as Lee pounced him, tearing at the rest of his clothes, teeth marking him, over and over.

"Baby." His hands felt like claws, both of them on Lee's back, his ass, nails digging in.

"Uh-huh." Those teeth scored his chest, the heat zinging up his body.

Humping up against Lee, feeling their naked skin rub together, Aaron bit at Lee's neck, growling. Worrying the spot until there was a bruise rising up.

Their cocks lined up, just perfect, Lee sliding from base to tip, over and over.

That made him want to howl. The only reason he held it in was because it would set off every dog in the place. Instead, he just pushed right back, growling a little.

"Yeah. More." Those fuzzy balls nudged against him, bumping him hard.

"Love." They rolled, and he pushed down against Lee, needing more friction. Harder. Faster.

"Uh-huh." Their mouths crashed together, the kiss hard enough to draw blood.

Goddamn. Soon. He was gonna just explode. Boom.

Claws dragged down his side, hard enough to sting.

Crying out, his whole body arching hard, Aaron came, his cock jerking alongside Lee's. Jesus, that was... It was just what he needed.

Lee wasn't far behind, humping and laughing, just fucking joyous as he came too.

Aaron took a kiss, humming, stroking all of the hot skin he could reach. "Better, baby?"

"Fuck, yeah." Lee chuckled, rubbing their noses together. "Let's order pizza and beer."

"You got it, baby." He was feeling damned good about the day, about mending things with Abby. Hell, he was feeling well fucked, too. Time to get to the rest of Lee's reward.

"Mmm." Lee petted his belly, grinned at him like a fool. "All meat."

"Yep. We'll get the Noah's Ark."

Then they'd work on getting Abby to come and play.

***

Abby lifted her hand, knocked on the heavy, heavy door, the rap of her knuckles barely making a sound. Inside, though, what sounded like ten thousand dogs started howling and barking and she took a few steps back, off the porch.

Oh.

Maybe this was a bad idea.

Maybe she could just leave the bottle of wine and the box of brownies and go.

Of course, just as she was about to turn and run, the door opened, and most of the dogs quieted down. It wasn't Aaron, though.

"Uh. Hi. I. Uh. Yeah." Jesus. Duh. She was just stupid.

"Hey, there. You must be Abby. I'm Lee." A big, square hand reached out to her, a smile lighting up pretty, light brown eyes.

"Oh. Hi. Yeah. I'm here for supper and to meet your crew."

Oh, Lee was just as fine as could be...

"Well, come on in, honey. Aaron was just taking the rest of the mutts out to the kennel so you wouldn't have them all jumping on you."

"Oh. Oh, that's good." She'd been okay with the dog, Baby, but jumping on her?

God.

"Can I take anything for you?" His hand still wrapped around hers, warm and firm, comforting. Just like Aaron's.

"I brought wine and brownies. I hope that's okay."

The house was nice - homey and big, not fancy at all.

"Oh, better than. Aaron!" He stepped back to let her in, and Aaron came in from the back, smiling at her.

"Hey, Abby."

"Hey. How's it going?" She could hear the dogs, the sounds easing up.

"Good. Good. Are those brownies?" Aaron looked so pleased, just smiling and coming to give her a hug.

"They are." Oh, he smelled good - male and

51

strong and sort of soapy. "How're you?"

"You just asked that." Aaron kissed her cheek, making her shiver.

"Oh, god. Sorry. I'm just..." She leaned in close, whispered in his ear. "I'm a little wigged out and you smell ready good and... You make me a little goofy."

Maybe a lot goofy.

Damn.

"Yeah? Oh, honey..." For a moment she thought he might kiss her, right there in front of his friend.

"Uh-huh." Damn, she was all blinky and starry-eyed and shit.

He did kiss her cheek before sliding a hand under her elbow and leading her to the couch. "Sorry about the dog hair. We tried to clean up, but we got a double golden retriever drop off this morning."

"Oh? You let them in the house even when you don't know them?"

Aaron and his friend exchanged glances. "We know these two, hon. They're working with us on obedience."

"Yeah? Like sit and stay and stuff? I've always wondered, do they understand words, really?"

"They understand well enough. Some better than others." Another sideways smile passed between the two men.

"Cats don't." She looked around - there were dozens and dozens of pictures of different dogs, big ones, small ones. There was one - a huge silver wolf with the prettiest eyes. She reached out, touched the frame.

"Beautiful, isn't he?" Lee said, smiling at her, reaching out, his fingers sliding over hers.

"Yes. Yes, he's... stunning." It was the truth. "The second one I've found beautiful in my whole life."

"Which was the first?" Oh. Lee moved so close

that his breath brushed her ear.

"There was this one he brought to Deb's." Fuck, her nipples were hard, aching. "Baby."

"Oh, you liked him, huh? I know he liked you a lot." One hand curled around her waist, Lee pressing up against her side.

"Yeah? He was... he wasn't scary." This had to be. She couldn't. Aaron was gonna wig right out.

"No, I know he didn't want to scare you." His lips trailed along her neck, warm and good.

"Oh..." She shivered, everything inside her going tight and hot.

"Now, Lee." Aaron moved up on her other side, his hand meeting Lee's at her waist. "You have to stop monopolizing the lady."

"I..." Oh, fuck her, this was getting altogether too fascinating. Intense. Hormonal. Something.

Aaron turned her slightly, lips sliding across her cheek and finally settled on hers, soft and hot. She'd never been in this position, but her body had definite ideas about what she wanted.

They got her moved, Lee behind her, Aaron in front, two big bodies rubbing against her. Their hands seemed to move in concert, sliding up and down her sides.

"I..." She went up on tiptoe, mind just swimming. What the *hell* was she doing?

"Shh. You're thinking loud, honey." Aaron smiled against her mouth. "It's okay. I promise."

"Yeah?" Somebody's fingers hit a hot spot and she shivered, gasped a little.

"Yes," Lee whispered in her ear from behind. "It will all be fine. Just feel."

She met Aaron's eyes, then he bent in and kissed her again, just stealing what little good sense she had left.

It was so easy to sink into the kiss, to let them

carry away her thoughts, make her shiver and moan. Her breasts felt heavy, her belly tight and hot. She couldn't quite catch her breath and her hands just slid up Aaron's arms, hanging on tight.

They both moved again, leaning her back against Lee's solid form, Aaron pulling her shirt up out of her jeans. Oh, his hands felt so good on her belly.

Lee's lips were on the back of her neck, the heat sliding down her spine, making her moan, go up on her tiptoes. Oh, god. So hot.

Aaron's hounds found her breasts, touching her through her bra. His fingertips slid down between the cloth and her skin, finding her nipples. Her butt rocked back against Lee, her nipples going hard as rocks.

"Sweet." Smiling, Aaron licked her lips. "You should taste, Lee. She's so damned sweet."

"Mmm. I can handle that. You okay, honey?" A hot, hot tongue slid over her neck, up toward her ear.

"I..." She shook, hanging on for dear life.

"It's all good," Aaron said, rubbing up against her, hips starting to rock.

"You're both... It's so hot." Two hard cocks, two hungry mouths - she was lucky.

"Uh-huh. Hot for you, honey. Huh, baby? Want her?" Wait. Baby?

"Mmmhmm. Pretty lady." She tried to focus. She did. But there were hands on her belly, on her breasts, just making her dizzy.

Lee moved back a little and Aaron's hands turned her and suddenly she was kissing Lee, Aaron rocking against her butt.

Lee's kisses were harder, a little sharper, and she sank into the pleasure, rocking between them. Aaron felt hot and huge behind her, his hands holding her hips to move her. Lee's hand slid across her hip and disappeared, but she heard Aaron moan.

Then Lee's hand pressed against her ass, sliding between her and Aaron. Oh. Oh, man. They. They were together. Like together-together.

Bone-meltingly hot.

"We need to sit down," Aaron murmured. He had a point. Her knees felt like Jell-O.

"Yeah. Collapsing here on the tile would suck." Oh. Go her! A whole sentence.

"Mmm. Couch is softer."

She felt like she was floating on air when they moved her, sort of working together to make it smooth and easy. Their hands slid all over her on the way, making it a sensual experience.

They settled, placing her between them, facing them, her legs spread over their thighs.

"Oh, Lee. Just look. Smell. She smells good with us, huh?" Aaron's hand pushed between her legs, his fingers pressing against the seam of her jeans.

She did her best not to blush, knowing she looked like a slut, spread between them and rocking against that touch.

"Beautiful." Lee smiled right into her eyes before leaning to kiss her. The move arched her back, offered her front right up to them.

Aaron took advantage of that, lips finding her nipple through her bra, teeth teasing her.

"So pretty." Lee helped ease her shirt all the way off, then attacked the clasp on her bra, helping Aaron out.

Lee wasn't bad at it, her breasts coming free, nipple just sort of popping into Aaron's lips.

Sucking strongly, Aaron flicked at her skin with his tongue. Lee's hand slid down, pushing under her jeans to feel her skin.

Abby had one hand on each broad, muscled chest, fingers sliding on their shirts, working open buttons.

"That's it, honey."

Lee sounded growly, just like Aaron had the last time. Hot. They were just stealing her breath and her inhibitions. She blinked, her whole rhythm caught in the suction at her breast, Aaron pulling and pulling. Lee undid her jeans, giving himself more room, and suddenly her focus shifted down. His fingers found her center, rubbing insistently.

"Oh." Her lips parted and she groaned, her skin going hot.

"She's wet, lover," Lee said just before taking her mouth again. Oh, God.

The kiss went deep and hot from the get-go, Lee's tongue fucking her mouth in the same rhythm as the fingers stroking her clit.

She became a circle of pleasure, from Aaron at her breast to Lee at her mouth, to both of them touching her beneath, Aaron's fingers sliding down to play against Lee's. Heat twined up her belly, flooding her, making her sob and twist, the pleasure sharp and amazing and overwhelming her.

"Shh. Hush, honey. It's okay." They moved together, tuning her so she lay across Lee's lap. Aaron pulled her jeans off, the scratch of them on her legs almost too much for her sensitized skin.

"Oh, god. I can't believe this is happening." She was wet enough that she'd be embarrassed if Aaron didn't almost growl, tongue sliding on her skin.

"Want you," Aaron said.

"So much," Lee agreed, both of them licking and nibbling at her.

"Yes." She nodded, right there with them, twisting under those strong hands.

Aaron's fingers slipped inside her, two of them, testing her. Lee bit at her neck, mouth hot and wet, tongue dragging roughly against her skin. Driving her crazy.

She bucked, face turned to rub against Lee. "Fuck. Fuck, please."

"What do you want, pretty lady? Aaron? Me?" His lips moved against hers, his breath warm, his hands moving over her.

"Does saying yes make me the biggest slut on Earth?"

"No." Chuckling, Aaron moved his fingers, making her shudder. "It means you're right here, with us, letting us love you."

"Oh, good. Then yes. Please. Multiple orgasms are a gift from God." She grinned, winked, pushed toward their touches.

"Yeah, honey. That's it." Laughing, Aaron kissed her again, his fingers slipping out. Lee handed over a condom, tanned fingers caressing Aaron's for a moment.

That was so hot. She moaned, eyes on where their skin touched. "Pretty."

"You like that, honey? Don't worry. There will be a lot more." True to his word, Aaron slipped the condom on, then lifted her up to straddle him. Lee moved in close behind her, Lee's hands on Aaron's thighs.

"More." She sank down, hands on Aaron's shoulders, that heavy, thick cock spreading her wide.

"Yeah. More." Lee kissed her shoulder, his fingers sliding up to pinch Aaron's nipples.

So hot. She started moving, riding nice and easy.

She could feel Lee, pressing against her bottom, hard and hot. When he leaned past her shoulder and kissed Aaron hard on the mouth she almost exploded into tiny pieces.

Her whole body shuddered and she shook with it, watching that kiss. Damn. Just. Damn.

"Come here, honey." Aaron was breathless when he pulled away from Lee, pressing in to kiss her, too, lips and tongue playing hers. He rocked up into her, filling her, even as Lee pushed her down to meet every thrust. Each little rush stacked on top of the last, making her pleasure go on and on. Both tongues were pushing in to taste her, to lick at each other.

Lee's fingers found her, right where she and Aaron joined, moving up the slightest bit. He worked her bundle of nerves unmercifully. She shattered, thighs so tight they hurt, hands squeezing whatever flesh they could reach.

Aaron growled like a great big wolf, pounding up into her, his whole body jerking beneath her. Lee went crazy, too, humping against her back, biting her shoulder hard enough to draw blood. Things got a little wild, a little weird, her orgasms coming in waves, the heat and growling and snarling exciting her unbearably.

When it was over, she lay on top of Aaron, stretched out along the couch, with Lee pressed up against their sides, licking where he'd bitten her. Every rasp of his tongue sent an aftershock of her orgasm through her.

"D...damn." She nuzzled in, lips tickled by the rough stubble on Aaron's throat.

"So sweet. You're so soft and sweet, love."

"Tasty, too." Lee's breath tickled her shoulder.

"I..." She laughed, feeling more beautiful than she ever had.

"Stay with us?" Aaron asked, and she had a moment where she would swear he meant forever. A moment where she could see it in his dark brown eyes. He couldn't mean it, but whatever he did mean, right now she nodded. Because right now, she meant yes.

***

The rest of the night with Abby had gone well. They drank wine and ate brownies out of the pan, naked as jay birds. They'd even gotten her to wear Lee's fuzzy old bathrobe and come out and watch while they fed the mutts.

Of course, when they woke up, curled together like two pups in a den, she was gone.

Aaron stretched, fighting the urge to get up and sniff all over the house to find her. She wasn't there. He would have heard her heartbeat.

He could smell the soap, the coffee - she must have gone off early. Lee hummed, rolling over, reaching for them.

Scooting up, Aaron took a kiss from Lee's half open lips, tasting Abby and his hot as hell mate. "Hey, baby."

"Mmm. Morning. Do I smell coffee?" Lee nuzzled in, licking a little, rubbing at him with morning wood.

"I guess? I think Abby made some before she left." Aaron grabbed that morning hard-on, thumb rubbing the tip.

"Work?" Lee's eyes rolled a little, tongue flicking out. "Mmm..."

"Maybe. I hope so." Aaron kissed Lee hard, concentrating on his lover instead of worrying about Abby.

Lee groaned for him, fingers in his hair and holding him close, giving him that muscled body to love on.

"Mmm. Baby. Love how hot you are for me." If he never had anything in his life but this man he would count himself lucky.

"Need you, hmm? It's okay." Lee looked right into his eyes, holding him. "She'll be back. Come on, fuck me."

"I'd like it if she does, but I love you, baby. You know that, right?" He reached for the lube, not about to turn that offer down.

Lee laughter settled him, down to the bone. His lover had no doubt about where they stood.

None.

Aaron grabbed the little tube, working it open, getting his fingers wet. "How do you want it, baby?"

"Hard and deep." That wink made him grin. Then, when Lee grabbed those knobby knees and spread wide, it made him groan.

"Hard. Deep. Got it." He could so do that. Right now. Turning, Aaron reached up between Lee's legs, sliding his fingers back until they slipped into that tight hole.

"Good dog." Lee started rocking, spine curled, pushing onto his touch.

"Bitch." He laughed, though, feeling like a king with Lee tight and hot around his fingers. He curled his fingers, searching for that little gland.

When he found it, Lee howled, toes curling up tight. "There. Damn. Again."

"Got you, baby." He wouldn't let Lee fall. He hit that little hot spot again and again, watching Lee writhe. Those little sounds made him hard enough to ache, and he pushed for more of them.

When Lee was moaning continuously and Aaron was fixing to pound nails with his cock, he finally pulled his fingers free and settled between Lee's legs, sliding right into that sweet hole.

"Fuck, yes!" Lee reached up and dragged him down for a bone-melting kiss.

"Uhn." Oh, God. He loved kissing Lee. Loved how it got toothy and amazing, how it made shivers go up and down his spine.

They found their rhythm, tongues and cock and ass and nails, everything just fitting.

Rocking, grunting, Aaron pushed harder, knowing Lee could take it, that he wouldn't break. Biting down on Lee's neck, Aaron slammed down, his cock about to just go off like a rocket.

Lee's cry rang out, ass clenching around his cock as heat sprayed over his belly. He let his head fall back, let his hips go crazy as he came, his hands clenching on Lee's hips. "Baby. Oh, God."

"Uh-huh." He got this great, goofy grin, Lee's tongue sliding over his jaw. "Not bad at all."

"Nope." He could snuggle awhile. They didn't have to feed for at least a half hour.

"Mmm. Make sure you call her, tell her to come back. We'll cook steaks."

"I will. She liked you, baby." Not in that, 'wow, we have so much in common' way, but in the 'man, you're hot' way.

"Mmmhmm. She liked both of us. We're fucking hot."

"You know it. Irresistible." He blew a raspberry on Lee's skin. "We need to feed. Moon's coming, too. We'll need to schedule Gil in."

"Yeah. I hear you." Lee stretched, creaking a little. "Man, I'm going to feel you all day."

"Good. Want you to be thinking about what I'm going to do to you tonight." Lee grinned, rubbing noses with him.

"Oh, cheating. So fucking cheating." He got his ass slapped, Lee laughing for him. "Up. Feeding. Work."

"Mmmhmm." He rolled out of bed and headed to the shower, humming under his breath. Abby would call. She'd have to, and if she didn't? He and Lee would just keep on playing by themselves.

***

Abby plopped down on the sofa, dust billowing up.

Good god.

She reached for the phone, dialed the number for the kennel. What a day.

"'Lo?" She knew that wasn't Aaron, so it had to be Lee. It couldn't be someone random, because the one tiny word sent shivers down her spine.

"Hey, Lee. It's Abby." If he said, 'who?', she was hanging up.

"Hey, there, honey." Oh, no. He knew who she was. "How are you doing?"

"Well, I... It's been a day. I... Can I ask you a question?" She curled her feet up under her.

"Sure, honey." She could hear barking, and then silence, so he must have shut himself off in another room. "What's up?"

"Well, this is going to sound stupid as hell, but... do you guys use some soap or shampoo that attracts dogs?" She run one hand through her hair, feeling like a huge idiot. "I mean, I know it's dumb, but, the dogs are jumping over fences to see me. Following me. There's dogs in the front yard, right now. And I showered at your house before I left for work."

"Soap..." He paused, and she could just hear him take a deep breath. "No, no soap. Dogs in the front yard. No shit?"

"I swear to God. Four of them. Staring."

"Huh." Another long silence stretched before he cleared his throat. "I don't think it was the soap, honey. Let me get Aaron and we'll come over."

"Huh? I mean, I'll just take another shower, but I could order a pizza, if you two want to come. Over."

A warm chuckle sounded, and she shivered,

remembering how his breath had felt on her skin. "Sure. Lover likes pizza. So do I. Just make it meat, huh? We'll be there soon."

"Okay, sure. See you in a few." She hung up, calling Mamma Mangia's and ordering two pizzas and a six-pack before running to shower with her own soap.

***

"I just don't get it, baby. Why would she be attracting male dogs?" Aaron drove toward Abby's, hands clenched on the wheel. "I could see females, with our pheromones."

"Uh. Well, I..." Oh, shit. Lee looked fucking *guilty.*

"What? Come on, baby. Tell me so I know before we get there." Damn it, he hated nothing more than being unprepared.

"I bit her. Hard."

"Oh, shit." A bite from a werewolf in human form wasn't always transmittable, but there was no guarantee that it wouldn't either.

"Yeah. I didn't mean to, man. I didn't. It just sort of happened and now..."

"Yeah. We'll have to see of she's just..." She could be carrying the infection but not be affected by it. Maybe.

"Well, are we just going to wait and see? I mean, she doesn't know about it. She's going to freak out."

"I don't know." Pulling to a stop in front of Abby's, Aaron surveyed the two labs, one great Dane and one little terrier mix who sat patiently, staring at her picture window.

Lee's hand landed on his thigh. "I'm sorry, man. Swear to god."

Aaron summoned up a smile. "It's okay, baby. I'm more worried than mad."

"Yeah, well..." Lee sighed, shrugged. "You want me to wait in the car?"

"No." He pushed his fingers through Lee's, squeezing. "I want you to come with me. We're together, you and me."

"Yeah? Okay. Okay. Let's go see for ourselves." They stepped out of the truck, the male dogs growling quietly, posturing.

Aaron drew up like a puffy frog, looking almost twice as big suddenly, and the dogs backed right down. One of them rolled to show his belly.

"Man, that is *so* hot." Lee grinned over, nudging him with one shoulder.

"Asshole." Chuckling, he went and rang Abby's doorbell, hoping she wouldn't be able to smell how Lee had made him hard.

"Coming!" She'd just showered - her hair was wet, thin t-shirt and shorts clinging to her curves. "Hey. Pizza's here."

"Cool. Hi, honey." He pushed in fast enough to make sure none of the dogs came in with him and Lee.

"Hey." He did love her house, with the heavy plants, the light everywhere. "Come on in. How's it going?"

"Good." Giving her a kiss, he nudged her toward Lee, who took her mouth, too.

"Oh." She pressed in for a second, smiling at them. "That was nice. Did you see that some the dogs left? I showered. I knew it was your soap."

"Uh-huh. Pizza smells good." Glancing at Lee, Aaron led her toward the kitchen, scoping out the rest of her house.

"I got meat." She had thrown paper plates on the table and the beer was in a bucket of ice. He could see the bite mark on her shoulder, the edges dark under the white shirt.

It made him want to jump on her and rub all over her. With Lee. Right now. Aaron held back by force of will only.

"You okay?" She looked back over her shoulder, damp hair falling down out of its loose ponytail.

"Uh." Clearing his throat, he adjusted himself, Lee's low chuckle making him growl.

Then a soft, full breast pushed against his arm. "Aaron?"

"I'm fine." Giving in to the urge, Aaron swung her around in front of him and bent to kiss her like he really wanted to. She opened right up, the kiss tinged with a hint of wildness, the scent of her irresistible. God, he could just eat her up. Lee must have felt the same, because he moved right up behind her, pressing Abby against him, lips falling right to the bite mark on her shoulder.

A hungry little cry pushed into his lips and her hips rocked in a motion old as time. Goddamn.

"Mmm." It came out as another growl. He couldn't help it. She was so theirs. Now they just had to get her to understand it, not freak out.

She pressed closer, nipples hard where they rubbed against his chest. Groaning, he bent to kiss each one, pushing Abby back against Lee. He needed her naked. Pizza could wait. Her shirt came up and off easily, the shorts sliding down like nothing so he could touch her.

Oh, so damned pretty. His hands came up, lifting her breasts easily, his thumbs rubbing. Lee leaned over Abby's shoulder and begged a kiss, and Aaron gave that, too. Abby leaned back, head on Lee's shoulder, and watched them, moaning low. They broke for air, and he grinned at her. "You like that, don't you, honey? Like to see me and Lee together."

Her cheeks went pink, but she nodded, licked her lips. "You're hot. Both of you."

"So are you," Lee murmured, lips sliding against her cheek. "So hot, honey."

He nodded, grabbing one of her legs up to wrap around his lip. Aaron groaned, cock trying to get to her, her wet heat evident even through his jeans.

"We should see your bedroom, honey. No dogs here to eat the pizza off the counter while we wait." Look at him, being all coherent.

"My sheets are clean." She backed away, bare ass shaking as she led them down the hall.

They followed like a pair of hounds on a scent, leaning on each other, Lee's arm around his waist. He copped a feel of Lee's ass, moaning a little. God, Aaron loved his life. Of course, she bent over that pretty, made bed to tug the comforter down and her legs spread and... Uhn.

Lee got there before him, pressing up against her round ass, rubbing like crazy. God, that was fucking hot, too. Her back arched, pushing back, head thrown back, lips open.

Lee was groaning, pushing against her, and Aaron was torn. Naked Abby. Still dressed Lee. He went for Lee, reaching between them to undo Lee's jeans and yank them down.

Lee gave a thankful little bark, leaning forward to bite at Abby's shoulder, her neck, cock pushing against her folds. He tore at Lee's shirt, too, just because he could. So he could touch that hot skin. Oh, damn.

The scent of them together made him want to howl, strong and fierce and feral. They rocked, his cock pushing at his pants, trying to get to Lee. He ripped his jeans open, slipping and sliding.

Lee growled as soon as his cock touched that hot, slick skin.

Reaching around Lee's lean hips, Aaron positioned Abby as best he could, pulling her up so Lee's cock pushed against her wet folds.

Lee groaned, hips rolling and pushing in deep. Abby's cry rang out and he damn near shot, just like that. Gritting his teeth, he held on, grabbing his own prick and pushing it against Lee's hole. He needed in, right in where it was hot. God.

"Now. Now, love." Lee pushed back against him, opening up and spreading to take his cock in.

"Now." Sliding right in, Aaron moaned, his hands on Abby's skin. She was so soft, Lee was so hard and hot... He thought he might explode.

"Oh, boys. I... Wow." Abby moved and Lee moved and he almost screamed.

"Honey. Baby." He sounded like an old Motown record, only with growling.

He could see the teeth marks on Abby's skin, Lee's marks. Aaron's balls drew up, and he cried out, his hips snapping. He held on by the skin of his teeth, wanting Lee and Abby to be right there with him. He could see the dull flush crawl up Abby's spine, her fingers curling into the sheets.

"Lee. Come on, baby. Help me out." He growled it in Lee's ear, wanting help to get them all together.

Lee groaned, leaned down and bit her nape, teeth grabbing her skin. Abby just melted for them, crying out, her whole body shaking. That was all they needed. Lee squeezed down around him, so tight it almost hurt, and Aaron lost it. He came hard, teeth clenching, hands clamping on Lee's skin.

They just swayed a minute, panting, rocking together before he slid to one side, landing on the mattress.

Lee brought Abby right down with them, gently, chuckling. "Pizza anyone?"

"Mmm. Pizza." Abby's stomach growled and they all started laughing.

"Let's eat." Aaron stripped off the rest of his clothes before hoisting his ass up and padding off toward the kitchen.

"My clothes are in the living room. God. You two are something else." He could hear Abby's voice, Lee's laughter.

"We're not having clothes for supper, honey," Lee said, all but dragging Abby to him like a bone.

"I know. Dorks." Abby was chuckling, breasts bouncing. Man, that was fascinating.

They both stood there and stared until she shifted from foot to foot. "What?"

She leaned down, grabbed her shorts, then her shirt, arms going up, which made her boobs do it again.

"You're... jiggling." Lee sounded like he loved the jiggling as much as Aaron did.

"What? Where?" She stopped, shirt half-down, looking.

"It's a good thing." Aaron smacked Lee's ass. You didn't tell a woman that way; they always thought it meant fat.

She looked over, then got it, her cheeks going red. "Well... they sort of stick out..."

"They do. It works very well." Aaron smiled, grabbing the pizza box and getting everyone a slice. Now that Abby was covered a little, his mind was more on that bite mark.

"Thanks." Abby opened three beers, handing them out.

Crisis averted. They all got a plate and headed for the couch, cuddling together in a puppy pile. "So, are you feeling okay, honey?"

"Hmm? Yeah. Yeah, it was a weird day - there were dogs everywhere following me. And I guess the treatment's really working because I just wasn't scared."

"Yeah. I would say you've hat the best treatment there is for that." Aaron glared at Lee. He was going to kill the man.

"Between you two and Deb, it's been amazing." Uh-huh. Like Deb did it.

"Well, good. So you feel a lot better about being closer to big animals..."

"Well, somehow I don't see myself running into any bears."

"No. No bears." Lee looked at him over her head. "What about wolves?"

"They're almost extinct, aren't they? Especially in the wild." She shrugged. "I don't know. Right now, it just doesn't *sound* scary."

"Oh, that's good." Lord, this was harder than he'd thought it would be.

"Is everything okay?" She looked from him to Lee and back, chewing her lip. "Is this like the gentle, gee, you're cured, we're moving on talk?"

"Nope." Lee turned, eyes clear, serious. "We don't want to move on, honey."

"Then what? You both look so... worried."

Aaron sighed. "Well, Lee bit you." Might as well just come out with it. She was gonna think they were crazy.

"Yeah. A little rough but..." Her eyes went wide. "You don't have... I mean. We didn't use a condom and... Oh, God."

"No, no." Lee soothed her with voice and touch, the low, easy sound like a chuff, just like a momma wolf with a cub. "It's not AIDs or Herpes or anything."

"Then what? What's wrong? You're scaring me." Her eyes were wide and he couldn't help but reach for her.

"Lee and I, we're unique, honey." He held her, feeling her shiver. "I... You remember Baby?"

"Yeah..."

Pretty, pretty boy. "That was Lee."

"What?" She stared at him, face blank. "I'm scared, not stupid."

Sighing, Lee moved closer, hand on her leg. "It's true, honey. I... we can change. That picture in the house? That's Aaron."

"What? What are you two talking about?"

"What we're trying to say is that we're werewolves, honey." Okay, she would either pass out or slap him. Or cry.

He didn't expect that.

"Okay. You know where the door is. I'm... I need. Yeah. Night."

"Abby. Wait." He held out a hand, trying to get her to come back. She'd gotten up, yanked on the edge of her shirt, smoothing it. "We're not trying to make you feel like an idiot. Why do you think all those dogs were following you around?"

"I don't *know*! That's why I called! Why are you doing this?"

"We're going to have to show her, baby." Lee moved around to stand between Abby and the door.

"Show me what? Just go away! Quit being weird." She was panicking; he could smell it.

"Shh. Shh." Aaron knew a few sub-vocalizations would calm her some, would ease her down.

"What's happening? What's wrong with you?"

Lee sighed, hand on her arm. "Nothing. We're just different."

"We didn't mean to involve you in... in this part of our lives, honey. We just couldn't help it." Poor baby. She was just teetering on edge.

"I don't understand."

Lee looked at him. "I'll do it. You... deal, huh?"

"Okay." Aaron took two steps forward and wrapped his arms around Abby. "Just watch, honey."

She leaned back against him, and he took that as a positive sign.

Tightening his grip, he held on, waiting for Lee to do his thing. Thank God it wasn't really painful.

Lee shifted, limbs going lean, muzzle growing, canines sliding out. Abby stared, shaking against him, eyes huge.

"Shh. He won't hurt you. He won't." Lee was so damned beautiful. It made him want to howl. Abby keened softly, the fear flooding his nose. "No, no. It's Lee. It's Baby. You know him."

"Aaron. Aaron, what is going on?" Her knees buckled, her weight going heavy in his arms.

"He's changing, honey. I told you. I can do it, too." He took her to the couch, letting her sink down.

She drew her legs up, wrapping her arms around her calves and staring at Lee. Lee came over slowly, tail wagging, tongue lolling. He nudged her leg, whining a little, those pale eyes irresistible.

She reached out, tears still going, fingers shaking as she stroked Lee's muzzle.

"That's it. That's it, Abby. Come on, baby. Let her feel how soft you are." It was working. Aaron had to believe it was working.

"How... how can you..." Abby let Lee rest his head on her hands, rubbing his ears and cheeks on her palms.

"I can't explain it, honey. I mean, we really don't know how. We just do." Hell, Lee had been born that way. Aaron had been bitten. It just... it worked.

"Okay..." She swallowed hard, closed her eyes. "And me?"

"We don't know yet." That was the hardest thing

in the world to say, but it was true. They would have to wait and see.

"What do you mean? Do I need to see a doctor?"

"No, no." Aaron stroked Lee's ears. "It's not something a doctor can sure, honey. Not everyone who gets bitten becomes like us, though."

One of her eyebrows lifted and she stared at them. "Don't believe the extreme irony of this has escaped me."

"I don't." He didn't. Neither did Lee, the way he chuffed, tongue pushing out on a lupine laugh.

"Good." Abby looked at Lee. "I swear to God, if dogs start humping my legs, I'm going to blame you."

Lee pressed into his hand, tongue lapping at her palm.

Aaron cracked up, hugging her tight. "I think we might keep you, honey."

"I think... I think you might have to, huh?"

"Yeah. Yeah, we might, but it's not gonna be hardship." He took a kiss, knowing Lee would get a little growly, loving that low grr.

She opened up to him, the flavor of tears there, but fading. Aaron kissed her deep, letting everything fall away, hoping she could do that, too. They needed to touch. To love. Lee leapt up next to them, fur becoming skin, hands sliding up over her shoulders.

"Mmm. Hey, baby." Aaron turned to bring Lee into the kiss, tongues and lips meeting, hot and wet. Lee pushed into the kiss, fingers sliding into Abby's hair.

"Mmm." He wasn't sure who it was that moaned first, but soon they were all making low noises, encouraging each other on.

He felt Abby's shiver as she snuggled in, and he

was so fucking proud of her.

Such a beautiful lady. She would be one of them, even if she wasn't now. He knew it.

**

Deb grabbed the little bag with her croissant reaching for her triple non-fat latte with the other. Since Abby had stopped coming on Tuesdays, she had a great, gaping hole in her schedule, and she took every opportunity to get out of the office at that time and walk a little.

The caffeine didn't hurt.

She left the coffee shop, turning on the heel of her pretty new pink pumps and walking briskly down the sidewalk. When she turned the last corner on the way back to her office, she spotted two men and a woman, all holding leashes and walking a pack of very large, drooling dogs.

Really, if she didn't know better, she'd say it was Aaron and his dear assistant, Lee.

It couldn't be, though, because that would mean the curvy, blonde girl with them was Abby.

Surely Abby wasn't that far cured?

"Deb!" Aaron hailed her with a raised arm and a smile. "Hey, Doc, how's it going?"

Well, goodness. It was them. Gingerly making her way up to the drooling dogs, Deb smiled at them all. "Look at you all, out for a walk. What brings you down here?"

"Scent training. They have to be able to concentrate only on what we want them to." Aaron smiled, such a handsome thing, and patted one of the dogs on the head.

Deb looked to Abby, who seemed in fine spirits, not at all bothered by the giant beast she held. "All cured up, are we? I wondered why I hadn't seen you, my dear."

"I called your assistant to cancel, Deb."

Lee moved right up next to Abby and nudged her with his elbow. "She's good to go, now, aren't you, honey?"

Shaking her hair back off her face, Abby nodded, her smile bright as the daylight. "I am. I do miss you, though, Deb. Maybe we can have lunch sometime."

"That would be lovely. Are you sure you don't need my services anymore?"

The strangest look passed between Abby and the two men, one full of mischief and fondness, their eyes reflecting all of the shades of brown, from Lee's light gold to Abby's pretty sherry color to Aaron's almost black.

"No," Abby finally said, pulling her sitting dog up to all fours again, making ready to go back to walking. "I think I'm absolutely cured."

"Well, good. Good. See you later, darlings."

"Bye, Deb."

She watched them walk away, sipping at her latte. Really, Abby looked wonderful. Confident, happy.

Funny, though. Deb could have sworn Abby's eyes were green.

Running with the Wolf
Sean Michael

Prologue

She ran.

Her feet pushed against the loam, the dry grass, the ground pushing back against her, helping her, shoving her faster and faster.

The sounds all around her screamed, telling her to hurryhurryhurry.

Faster, faster.

Please, Victoria. Run.

There was the hint of blood in her mouth, the threat of dawn lightening up the sky. She was heading home -- home to the big house, to her studio, to the normal, easy rhythm of life that she'd lost in a rush of pain and cramp and moonlight.

Vicki hit the clearing, a monster snarling at her, its golden eyes freezing her to her spot as it growled and charged her. It nearly took her, too, except that she remembered to leap back, to snap at the air as it went by. The smoke billowing from it tasted oily, foul.

Monsters.

There was a box on the porch and she sniffed and snuffled around. Milk. Milk and cream and a plastic-bound promise of cheese.

Milk.

The night was fading and she nosed around, looking for somewhere to rest, to hide. Somewhere safe. Somewhere solid. Somewhere soft.

There was a blanket that smelled like her and she leapt up, fluffing it with her paws, her nose. Oh. Warm. Soft. Better.

Better.

The sky was turning light -- pinks and greens and blues like Easter eggs and little girl makeup and...

Vicki blinked, staring up into the dawn. Her hands slid down her sides, her stomach growling, dirt sliding from under her fingernails as her mind raced.

Why the hell was she out here on the porch?

Naked and filthy?

Cold?

Again.

Chapter One

There was a new wolf in their territory.

Dibs had found the scent first -- Dibs always found everything first. He had too much energy and not enough sense and always went full tilt at everything.

Swan couldn't remember ever being that young.

Dibs came barreling toward him, knocking him over and sending them both rolling, tongue hanging out and slobbering all over him. Swan growled and snapped and Dibs backed off enough for him to get back up on all fours. Three happy barks sounded and Dibs rubbed against his side, muzzle sliding along his own.

He gave another growl, but his heart wasn't in it. Dibs didn't mean any harm, he was just young and exuberant and the pup adored the hell out of him. And maybe, just maybe, he adored the hell back. Giving a soft yip, he licked at Dibs' muzzle, the young wolf vibrating and then barking happily. Dibs took off down a human path, came back and took off again.

Swan followed more slowly -- you never knew what you'd come across on the human paths and it was best to proceed with caution.

The path led out of the woods to a two story house with lots and lots of windows looking into the trees. Swan sniffed around and sure enough, the scent led from the woods to the house. Dibs was already bounding across the acre that separated house and woods and Swan barked sharply, calling Dibs back.

Whimpering, looking back at the house over and over, Dibs obeyed, lying down in front of him. Swan growled a warning; it was stupid to go where humans were while in wolf form. If he'd told Dibs once, he'd told the pup a million times.

He backed up out of sight, Dibs following with obvious reluctance. Clothes. Fetch. He barked the command and Dibs immediately barked and took off through the woods. They hid clothes in a small pack kept safely hidden near the entrance they usually used to leave the woods. Not that they did that often.

Swan didn't expect it to take long for Dibs to fetch it, but he moved off the path anyway, staying hidden in among the trees. A nice nap wouldn't hurt anything... He awoke some time later to Dibs pouncing him, the pup barking and laughing and jumping on him.

By Artemis' bow, he was too old for this.

He shifted, Dibs following suit and always, his eyes were drawn to the smooth skin with its dusting of hair, the lithe muscles, and the heavy cock nested in a riot of dark curls. Okay, maybe he wasn't too old.

Dibs' light blue eyes were twinkling and he was bouncing. "What do we do now?"

"Put your clothes on, pup, and try not to lick anything."

Dibs pouted, but did as he was told and soon they were both casually dressed. Dibs took off down the path again and by the time Swan had caught up, Dibs was on the back porch, trying to look in through the floor to ceiling windows.

"Dibs," he hissed. "We have to go around to the front."

"But this is where the scent ends."

"Yes, but civilized people prefer to have you go in through the front door. Come on!"

There were some days he thought perhaps a real house in town would have made sense, would let Dibs learn more fully about his human side. But the pup liked to run and he enjoyed his privacy, and the cabin in the woods did a fine job as a home for them, the land around it theirs by human law as well as pack law.

He gave Dibs a warning look as they climbed the front steps, and knocked on the door. Swan heard cursing and movement, then a heart-shaped face appeared in the doorway, a smear of paint on one cheekbone, a riot of black curls held back by a kerchief. "Can I help you?"

He could feel Dibs vibrating in place beside him. "She's pretty."

"Shh." He gave Dibs another look and then turned back and smiled, trying to keep it from being too toothy. Humans didn't like the toothy smiles. "Hello, there. Could we talk to you for a moment, please?"

"Look. I'm not buying anything, I don't need Jesus, and I have a gun and a headache, so if you're here for trouble, I'm the wrong girl."

Swan opened his mouth slowly, formulating a reply that wouldn't find them with the door slammed in their faces and the aforementioned gun at the ready. It appeared, however, that Dibs had spent his entire ration of patience and he bounded right up to her, and licked the woman's unpainted cheek, from jaw to eyebrow. "I'm Dibs!"

Artemis save him.

The door shut with a click, the sound of the lock turning simply huge. Excellent.

"Are you happy now?" he asked, shooting a glare at Dibs.

Dibs bounced and tried to see in the little window at the top of the door. "What?"

Swan shook his head and tugged Dibs away from the door. "Stand right here and don't move. You let me do the talking and you don't lick her! I told you not to lick anything."

"She's not an anything -- she's a she. And she's the wolf."

"Possibly."

"Couldn't you smell it on her? I could! She's one of us. She's the new one."

"Or her husband is, who is no doubt a very large, very strong man, and he's now got a possessive streak a mile wide as a part of his wolfish instincts..." What a mess.

"No, she said she has a gun." He just looked at Dibs, the pup vibrating with the effort to stay put. "If she had a husband, why would she tell us about the gun and not him?"

"Oh, for Artemis' sake... just stay there and no licking! None! Or you won't get to lick me when we get home."

Dibs' eyes went wide, but he did subside. Some.

Swan cleared his throat and knocked on the door again. "Hello? Hello? Please, we would just like to talk to you."

"Look, man. There's nothing you have to say that I need to hear. Don't make me call the sheriff."

"No, no. Don't call the sheriff. Look, my name is Swan and I live in the woods. I wanted to talk to you about... well, wolves."

He could see Dibs out of the corner of his eye, trying very hard to be still, and likely about to burst very soon.

"Wolves? Are you like some Green organization talking about my work, because I just went out to watch and take pictures for reference. I didn't mean to scare them and I just told the hospital that it was wild dogs." The door opened a crack, bright green eyes appearing again.

"No, we're not with any Green organizations. I'm not with an organization at all..." He was beginning to have an awful thought.

"Green?" piped up Dibs. "If a wolf's green there's something really wrong with it."

He shot a glare at Dibs. "You said you'd be good and stay still and quiet in your corner."

Dibs pouted, skulking in the corner of the little porch.

Swan smiled at the woman again. "You were bitten, yes? Not that long ago?"

"Yeah. Three months ago -- the beginning of summer." Her arm twisted, a mass of neatly stitched scars obvious.

"I'd like to talk to you about that if you don't mind. My companion and I live in the woods, you see... Oh, where are my manners." He held out his hand. "I'm Swan."

"I... Victoria. Vicki. I. I'm working..." Her nostrils flared, he could see it. Poor thing, her body had to be so confused. It was a hard enough transition for those not born to it, even harder if there was no one to walk you through it.

"Hi Vicki, may I say that it's very nice to meet you."

"I'm Dibs!" The pup bounded forward, but Swan managed to grab the back collar of Dibs' t-shirt, and hauled the pup up next to him.

"Yes, I believe we've already established that."

"Look. I'm sorry. I don't... Is he okay?"

Dib's eyes were wide, the pup pulling against his grip.

Grabbing at the straws her words offered, Swan shook his head. "He hasn't eaten since last night and low blood sugar makes him a little loopy." He hated lying, but if they could just get in, it would be much harder for her to kick them out when he told her what he had to tell her.

"Oh. Well. I could give you some lemonade.

Outside. On the patio." She pointed, the look firm.

"Around the back on the deck?" he suggested. It would be better if they did this as far away from the road and possible prying eyes as they could get. He let go of Dibs' shirt, and put his arm around the pup instead, drawing Dibs tight against him in warning. Miraculously, the pup stayed mum.

"Yeah, that's fine. I'll bring a tray out there." The door closed again, the lock turning.

Dibs immediately bounced away from him, heading down the stairs. "Lemonade? Do you think it will be nasty like lemons? Why would anyone want to drink something sour like that?"

"I have no idea, Dibs. But whatever it is, you will drink it."

"I won't! Not if it's nasty stuff!"

Swan grabbed Dibs arm as they rounded the corner of the house. "Now listen here. If you do anything else to screw this up I will take you home and beat you."

Dibs' eyes went wide and the scent of the pup's pheromones hit him like a ton of bricks. "Promise? Promise, Swan? Please."

He rolled his eyes. He. Was. Too. Fucking. Old.

And then Dibs kissed him, all eager limbs and mobile lips, tongue pushing into his mouth. "I'll be good, Swan, I promise. For you, love." And then Dibs was running, bounding out to the back of the house.

Oh.

Sweet pup.

Swan made his way more sedately, thinking of bears and traps and getting spider webs caught in your throat so that by the time he was climbing the stairs to the back deck, he no longer had an erection.

Of course, then Victoria stepped out, wearing a

little paint-covered man's shirt, a worn pair of jeans that hugged her curves and that had him hard again. Aching.

She had a glass tray with a pitcher of lemonade, a haphazard little pile of sweets - brownies and cookies and peanut butter crackers.

That was just what Dibs needed -- sugar.

There was nothing for it, though, and maybe Dibs would be subtle and keep his own hard-on hidden. Well, hopes didn't need to be logical, did they?

Swan sat in one of the chairs, crossed his legs and put his hands in his lap. "Than you, this is very kind."

"Oh, this is good stuff, this lemonade, Swan, I don't have to pretend to like it!"

Swan bit back his groan.

Victoria chuckled, the sound soft, gentle somehow. "No, you shouldn't have to pretend to like it at all."

"It's good! It really is." Dibs bounced where he sat and Swan couldn't help but smile indulgently.

"Is he your brother? I have a baby sister that is... full of energy."

"No, he's... my companion." There weren't words for what Dibs was to him. Friend, lover, mate. His. None of them were adequate.

"Oh. Cool." She sat back, nibbling on a cookie.

Dibs handed him a brownie. "You have to try one of these, Swan. They're awesome!"

He took the brownie and nibbled on the edge. It was good. He wasn't much of a cook -- they pretty much ate while in wolf form. "This is good." He had a bit of lemonade, too. "So... " How to get this back on track?

"Thank you." She drew her feet up underneath her and Swan caught sight of a strip of her stomach, soft and smooth. His eyes were caught momentarily and he had to shake himself. He wasn't a pup like Dibs, and shouldn't have been so easily distractible.

"The bite." Dibs poured himself more lemonade. "Ask her about the bite."

"Yes, of course. It happened three months ago, you say?" Three months of not knowing what was happening -- it would have driven him mad.

"Yeah. I told you, I didn't mean to spook them. I was taking pictures and one came around behind me."

"The bite healed properly? You didn't have any trouble with it? You wouldn't mind if I looked at it more closely, would you?" There had been a pack who'd traveled through his territory a few months back, they'd moved on, though, or he'd hunt them down and demand to know why they would bite a human and not take her in, teach her what she needed to know.

"It's fine. The ER doctor stitched it up, gave me the rabies treatment, antibiotics, the whole bit." She held out her arm, pushed the rolled sleeve up. "Please, the wolves are fine. I'm fine. I'd like to just leave it alone."

Swan took a gentle hold of her arm and slid his fingers over the scars. It was healing very nicely -- the scar probably wouldn't even be noticeable when she was in wolf form.

"Are you fine, though?" he asked. He knew very well she couldn't be. There would have been several days every month when she'd changed, though it was possible she didn't have any recollection of it. Her body would have protected her mind from something it couldn't possibly understand, not without guidance.

"Yes. Yes, of course. It's even stopped itching."

"You didn't have any one to lick it for you? That

would have stopped the itching ages ago!" Dibs had come around, and looked like he was about to demonstrate his remedy for the itching on the spot.

Swan shot the pup a look, hoping it was reminder enough that Dibs had promised not to lick anything else while they were here.

"Oh. I. Right. Okay. Are you feeling better, then, because I have work to do." She smelled scared.

"Sit down, Dibs." He worked to keep his voice calm for Vicki's sake.

Dibs did as he was told, the pup obviously having scented her fear as well.

"I just have one more question, if you don't mind." He continued without giving her a chance to say that she did mind. "Have you experienced anything strange in the months since you've been bitten? Strange feelings? Lost time? Unexplainable changes to yourself, or to your home?"

"What are you talking about?" Her face went milk-white pale and her glass clattered on the table.

He stroked her arm, seeking to soothe her, her panic clawing at him, demanding he do something about what was scaring her. "Not all wolf bites are equal and if you're going through strange changes, you don't need to be alone."

Dibs nodded enthusiastically. "We can help!"

"Help? I'm not sick. I'm fine. Honestly." Lies. Fear. A hint of sickness.

He took it as a good sign that she didn't pull her arm out of his reach. "I didn't say sick, but I imagine all is not right with you. There are strange things in this world, things that you may not even believe yourself."

"We can help! You can run with us in the woods -- running is so good!" Swan couldn't fault Dibs for trying to help in his own way.

"Okay. Okay, time for you and your friend to go.

It's been fun."

Swan sighed, but didn't argue. The full moon was coming, it always did. They would come back then.

"It was good to meet you, Vicki. Thank you for your hospitality." He stood and held out his hand to her, wanting to leave things on a positive note.

Dibs smacked his hand away, glaring. "We can't go! She needs us! Vicki needs us!"

"No. No, I don't. You two have a good afternoon. Take as many of the brownies as you want."

Dibs' eyes lit up and he reached for the sweets, but Swan grabbed his arm. "No, thank you for your kindness, though. Come along, Dibs. We have taken up enough of this lady's time."

"Vicki -- her name is Vicki." Dibs tugged against his hold, obviously not wanting to go.

"Vicki would like us to leave, Dibs and so we must, so she knows we are reasonable and that we listen to her, hmm?"

Dibs sighed, all his bounce disappearing. Swan wasn't worried -- he knew it would be back. In spades.

"Bye Vicki," Dibs said softly.

"Bye." The back door closed, the pretty lady heading for the stairs.

Swan took one last look and headed off the deck toward the forest. Dibs bounded after him, stopping him. "We're really going?"

"Do you see a choice?"

"We have to make her understand!"

Swan shook his head. "She's frightened of what's happening to her, and of us. We'll come back during the full moon."

Dibs was quiet a moment, stopping him again when they'd reached the edge of the woods. "What if she still wants us to go away, then?"

"I don't think she will, but we'll cross that bridge when we come to it."

"Okay. Can we shift?" Dibs was bouncing again, muscles vibrating.

"We need to get far enough in, take off our clothes and put them into the backpack, hide it again. Then we can change."

Dibs rolled his eyes, and grabbed Swan's hand. "Come on, then -- I want to run! I want you to think about beating me." Then Dibs swatted his ass and ran ahead, laughing.

Swan shook his head following, moving quickly. Maybe he was too old for this, but Dibs kept him young, kept him happy, and that was what mattered. He glanced back at the house, just barely making it out through the thickening trees. For now.

Chapter Two

Dibs ran and ran and ran and ran and ran.

And ran.

And then he ran some more.

Running was good.

Running was the goddess' best gift.

He ran past the cabin and slowed down when he noticed Swan sitting, in man form, on the swing on the porch, and circled back.

Running was the goddess' second best gift.

He bounded up to Swan, and sat on the man's feet, tongue lolling out, nose twitching happily at the smells of home and want and Swan. He'd change -- he would, loving in man form with Swan was amazing! -- but first he wanted petting and scritches which were almost as good as running.

"Dibs." Swan smiled down at him, leaning down to bury those long fingers in his fur. "You've been busy. Did you go over to the glass house again?"

He barked once. Of course he had. Someone had to look out for pretty Vicki. He wondered what her fingers would feel like in his fur -- would they be as good as Swan's, which currently had him drooling.

Dibs butted his head up when Swan's fingers slowed and encouraged them to scratch behind his right ear, just... oh yes, there. Swan chuckled, fingers sliding down to tease him, rub and scratch just like his needed. Soft words poured down around him -- telling him he was good and smart, fine and strong.

He whined happily, enjoying the petting and praise for a long time before slowly changing, fur becoming skin, muzzled becoming mouth, body stretching, so naked without his fur.

"Mmm. Good evening." Swan's voice moved over him like a touch.

"Swan!" He bounced up and pounced Swan,

straddling Swan's legs and making the swing sway wildly.

"Yes, I do think I am your Swan." He got a smile, Swan tugging him down into a wild, hungry kiss, tongue pushing into his lips.

He held on, already rubbing against Swan's lean, whipcord strong body. Oh, yes, the best gift, this. Them. Together.

They found a rhythm -- boom, boom, boom. Swan's body responded, cock hard against his.

"In me! In me! In me!" Each time he said it a little louder, his body rocking into Swan's. He liked that the best.

"Pup." Swan nipped his bottom lip, tugged it hard enough to sting.

He growled a little. "Yours."

Swan's eyes widened, passion growing. "Prove it, pup."

His nostrils flared as he picked up the scent of Swan's need and he rose up on his knees, reaching back for Swan's hard cock. Swan bared his teeth, hips rocking up toward his touch. Moaning, he guided Swan's cock to his hole, pressing back the next time Swan rocked up.

The heavy shaft pushed into him, piercing him, filling him up with a single, long thrust.

"SwanSwanSwanSwan!" It was good, so good. Running was a far-far distant second best gift.

He started to ride, rising up on his knees and pushing back down onto Swan's cock. Yes! Swan panted into the curve of his neck, tongue lolling out, licking at him. It was bigger than their whole forest, what he and Swan had together.

Dibs bounced on the hard cock, loving it. Their sounds rang out, both of them eager and hungry for it.

"Touch me!" he demanded, leaning in to lick at

Swan's neck, from collarbone to jaw line.

That firm hand grabbed his prick, stroking it in long, smooth strokes. He didn't have any words anymore, or he would have shouted them. Instead he licked and bit and howled out his pleasure. Swan's cock throbbed in his ass, heat flooding him in sudden pulses. Yes! Yes! Yes!

Dibs kept bouncing, wrapping his hand around Swan's and in seconds he was coming, too. Swan growled for him, soft and happy, hands sliding down his back. He pressed in close, cuddling and snuffling at Swan's neck. Swan smelled good, right. It made him happy.

"Mmm. Mate. The moon is beginning to call."

"I know! I can feel it. So pretty up in the sky and calling. Calling -- Dibs! Come and play!"

"Mmm. Dibs, play with your Swan!"

"Yes! Yes! Now!" Laughing, he threw himself backward, Swan's prick sliding from his body.

He'd changed before he hit the porch floor, barking for Swan to come! Swan rolled his eyes, but the big body shifted, paws hitting the ground with a thump.

Dibs put his head back and gave a little howl and then pounced Swan, rolling them out into the grass. Swan's teeth caught his tail, tugging a bit before Swan loped off, daring him to follow.

Barking and leaping, he did, bounding after his Swan.

So good. So happy.

Chapter Three

She threw the paint on the canvas, the red and blue splashing, dripping down, sliding over one another.

The moon was coming up over the trees, nearly full, and Vicki's skin was itching, burning, trying to crawl off her bones. Goddamn it. She was fucking tired of this... this... weirdness.

This hurting.

She needed to go see her doctor again. Or something.

There was a knock on the back door, the glass rattling in its frame. Vicki screamed, jumped and dropped her paintbrush. Fuck. Fuck.

The knocking got louder, accompanied by shouting. "Are you all right in there?"

"Yeah. Yeah, just a second." She grabbed her brush off the floor, dunked it into a tub of turpentine and headed downstairs. "Who is it?"

"Swan and Dibs. We met you earlier in the month?"

Oh, great. The crazy guy and the growly guy. "I'm all out of brownies."

"We can help!" That was the crazy guy.

"Dibs is right, Vicki. Please."

"Look, guys. I will call the sheriff. I'm sorry, but you have to go." This was just... weird. Her eyes were caught by the moonlight, peeking over the tops of the trees.

Swan turned to look as well, Dibs just vibrating beside the older man. "The change is coming, Vicki. It will be easier with someone who knows what's happening to guide you.

"Change? What change? Look, just go away. I have to work." To paint.

He scratched at the glass door. "Please. Let us in.

Or come out. Come out. I know you can feel it coming." There was an urgency to his words.

She shook her head, hand reaching for the door. No. No, nothing's coming.

Dibs bounced up in front of Swan, eyes wide and wild. "You have to come with us, Pretty Vicki. The moon is calling!"

"Go home. Please." She stumbled backward, tripping over the tiles.

"Break the door, Swan! Break it down, she's hurting herself!" Swan banged on the glass again.

"I'll call the police!" She whirled around, confused. A weapon. She needed a weapon.

Itchy. Christ.

"You won't be able to call anyone in a minute. Or get out without breaking the glass. Has that happened before? Have you woken up with glass all over the floor?"

Dibs kept bouncing, and now he was pulling at Swan. "It's coming, Swan. It's coming!"

"GO AWAY!" Vicki couldn't breathe, stumbling forward as her heart pounded.

"Break it, Swan!"

"Stand back," Swan shouted at her. And then he backed up and came at the door, shoulder first.

Oh, God.

Oh, God.

She turned to run, to lock herself in the bedroom when the world went upside down.

The sound of glass shattering was loud. Louder still were the growls and barks, but at the same time they were somehow soothing. Scrambling, she ducked into a dark shadow, panting with the need to run, to bite.

There were two wolves in the room, one large and solid, the other smaller, but moving, barking. She groaned as a wave of pain caught her, her claws scrabbling on the tile. The large wolf whimpered and growled softly. She scooted backward, deeper into the shadows, into the dark.

The smaller wolf bounded toward her, the bigger one growling. The noise didn't stop the eager wolf, though, and he came right into her dark corner, barking at her. She whimpered, scrambling back, paws sliding.

Both wolves started barking, the smaller one still coming toward her, the bigger one seeming angry. Her backend hit the wall and suddenly the wolf was right in front of her, muzzle rubbing along hers.

She let out a harsh, scared noise, eyes rolling.

The muzzle rubbing turned into a soft licking, the wolf whimpering softly. The touch soothed her and she took a deep breath, blinking. The wolf gave a little yip, the licking continuing. The other wolf came near slowly, a low, soothing rumble sounding deep in his chest.

Her head ducked, a soft sound leaving her chest. Scared. She was so scared. The wolves stood on either side of her, rubbing and rumbling and licking. She shouldn't have, but she felt safe between them. They smelled good -- like forest and wind and such.

The smaller one gnawed on her ear, the bigger one chuffing -- laughing. She nudged the smaller male away, shaking her head. Hungry. So hungry.

He barked and then bounded away, stopping at the door and looking back, barking. The larger wolf barked as well, nudged at her hindquarters.

No.

No. She couldn't go out there.

It wasn't safe.

The young wolf bounded back to her barking, and then ran back to the door, leaping over the glass and landing gracefully on the deck. There was a sharp nip to one of her hind legs. She stumbled forward, surprised, snarling a little as she lost the safety of the shadows.

The smaller one put his head back and howled at the moon, the sound touching her deep inside, even as another nip came to her hindquarters. She took another step, sniffing so hard it ached, a rumbling need growing inside her.

Nudging her again, the wolf behind her was quite insistent. The wolf on the deck stopped howling, barked twice and then bounded off, running toward the trees. She caught herself following, giving chase with a happy bark. The moon! The moon!

The larger wolf stayed behind her, no longer nipping at her, but barking and running as they gave the smaller wolf chase through the trees. The trees were tall, dark, hiding the moon away and the smells just fascinated her.

The smaller wolf came barreling back to her and the larger male, barking and happy and telling her how good it was to run and how she had to come now! She laughed and pounced, rolling the smaller male before strutting off.

She could feel the laughter of the larger male, hear it like a song, while the smaller wolf bounced up and pounced her from behind, sending them rolling again. He was larger than her, even if he was the smaller of the two, and she tumbled, landing on her side with a thump.

The bigger male barked and growled, pouncing the smaller wolf and slamming him to the ground. The smaller one snarled and snapped, but the bigger male growled again. Putting his head back, the smaller one submitted, the larger male's teeth closing around the vulnerable neck

Then it was over and the smaller one was running again, yipping happily.

She stared, stepping back under some scrub brush, swallowing hard. The larger male came to her, nuzzling, gentle. Her heart pounded, nose wrinkling as she sniffed. A low rumble sounded and her face was licked, the male leaving his scent on her.

She head-butted him, calling softly. So good. He smelled so good. He chuffed and butted back, muzzle open as he used it to rub hers. She licked his chin, his muzzle, tasting. He allowed it, a low, pleased rumble sounding.

And then the smaller one was back, bounding and pouncing on them, sending them both down, before taking off, fast. The bigger male barked and took off, giving chase.

She chuffed and followed, the leaves crackling under her feet.

They were led on a merry chase, the smaller male amazingly fast. Every now and then they'd be almost upon him and he'd put on a burst of speed, his barking laughter coming back to them on the wind.

She slumped down when she got tired, lapping at her paws, watching them run. Every now and then they'd come by and stop to pounce or lick her, and then they were off again.

The larger wolf tired first, joining her while the smaller male kept running, disappearing and reappearing until the moon began to give way to dawn. Then the bigger male nudged at her, encouraging her to get up.

She stood, head turned toward the lights at the edge of the forest. Home. She needed to go home.

The male was encouraging her to go in the opposite direction though, growling softly. And the smaller male kept running off, then coming back and barking urgently

She whimpered, muzzle pointing to the den with the lights. Home.

Her flank was nipped again, the bigger male trying to get her to go in the other direction. It was impossible not to follow; everything in her insisted that she follow the Pack leader.

The two males hurried her along, running deeper into the forest until they came to a small clearing with a log cabin. She barked, circling the place, unsure.

The males ran for the porch, curling up together and giving her a twin pair of barks. The moon was all but gone and she could feel something happening to her.

She stumbled forward, exhausted, worn bone deep. Home. Home.

They helped her up the stairs and when her body betrayed her, muscles screaming, they curled around her, fur warming her.

All she could do was sleep and wait for the morning.

Chapter Four

Once the moon had set and the sun rose, Swan shifted long enough to get a blanket from the cabin, spreading it over Vicki's naked body and Dibs' sleeping form. Then he let the wolf have him again and he stood guard, sitting at the edge of the porch and guarding his pack.

Ears and eyes and nose were all working hard, capturing each sound and sight and smell, analyzing them, categorizing threat levels.

The pup woke first, bounding over to give him love, rubbing their muzzles together. Then Dibs went over and sat next to Vicki, helping him guard

Her pretty green eyes popped open, went huge as she saw him and Dibs. Fear and panic flooded the air and Vicki stood, wrapping the blanket around her.

He called out to Dibs and let himself change. "Don't be afraid," he told her, his voice rough.

"Oh, my God." She stepped backward, swallowed hard. "I've lost it. I've finally lost it."

"It's all right, Vicki. It's Dibs and Swan from the other day. Everything will be all right."

Tears made her eyes shine and her mouth opened and closed, over and over. Dibs whimpered and went right up to her, not bothering to change, just rubbing against her.

"Please." She jerked away and began to run, stumbling into the trees.

Dibs ran after her, barking.

"Change you fool!" he called out, running as well, his longer legs catching up to them. He grabbed her arm and she spun around, making it easy to gather her in close. "Shh. Shh. There now."

"I. I. I can't. I..." He could hear her heart pounding violently, feel her throat working.

Dibs, finally in human form, touched her cheek. "Don't be scared, Vicki. You ran with us last night -- don't you remember? It was wonderful!"

"I. I don't." Her eyes rolled wildly and Swan knew they were losing her, that that was all too much.

He put his arm around her shoulders so he could catch her if she fainted, and then he licked her lips, giving her his scent, hoping the animal instincts that were buried inside her now would recognize his scent.

"Hey! You licked her!"

He ignored Dibs' indignant words, looking into Vicki's eyes.

Her lips parted, eyes fastened to his, so he licked again, breathing into her, flooding her with the scent of Pack. Dibs pushed close and licked her lips as well, and his, giving him a defiant glare. He would have laughed, but for not wanting to spook Vicki.

"It's us," he said softly. "You're safe, I promise."

"I'm scared."

"You don't have to be scared," Dibs said, pressing in close from the other side. "Swan and I'll keep you safe and Swan is so good at taking care -- look at how good he's taken care of me!"

Swan smiled at Dibs and then looked into Vicki's eyes again. "I know you don't understand what's going on. The wolf who bit you should have stuck around, should have made sure you understood the changes."

If that pack ever crossed their territory again, he would have some very strong words for them. And he would chase them away.

"Changes?" She shivered, stepped closer. "I'm cold. Where are my clothes?"

"Do you not remember any of it at all?" Swan

wrapped both arms around her and encouraged Dibs to press close from the other side, warming her.

"I... I remember the moon?"

"Yes, yes, the moon brings about the change." He looked at Dibs and nodded back the way they'd come. His pup understood what he wanted and together they began to move back toward the cabin. It was far closer than Vicki's house.

"I. What change?" Her cheek pressed against his shoulder.

"This is going to sound a bit fantastical," he admitted. "The wolf that bit you was not an ordinary wolf but a werewolf."

"Like us!" Dibs declared.

"What?" She stopped, stared. "Stop it."

"Stop what?" he asked.

"I didn't do anything!" Dibs said.

"Stop trying to fuck with me! Stop trying to scare me! Where are my fucking clothes?"

Swan's back stiffened. "We are not fucking with you or trying to scare you. We are trying to help you. Now come with us to our cabin and you can borrow something to wear. Then we can guide you back through the forest to your house."

"Uh-oh," Dibs whispered loudly. "You've ticked him off."

"Ticked him off? What? You two come to my house, scare me, I wake up here naked and I'm supposed to be nice? Oh, wait. Right. I'm a fucking vampire or something? I..." She wrenched away, tears rolling down her cheeks, the sun lighting her pale skin to gold. "I'm leaving."

"We have been nothing but honest with you. And I know it's a lot to take in, but it is the truth and we would like to help you. I am not in the habit of scaring women."

"You're not in the habit of doing anything to

women," the pup put in.

"Oh, shut up, Dibs!" He growled impatiently. This wasn't a problem of his making and it would have been so much easier to just let her go, let it go and stay buried deep in the forest.

He couldn't, though. She needed him and Dibs both. Whether she knew it or not.

Dibs whimpered and backed away, making him growl more. "Show her," he suggested, knowing that Dibs was dying to shift and run off his hurt feelings.

"Watch," he told Vicki. "Watch Dibs closely."

She wrapped her arms around herself, shaking violently. Dibs shifted, turned into the beautiful, strong wolf.

He was admiring his mate when he heard the dull thud of Victoria's body hitting the ground.

Chapter Five

Dibs started barking as soon as he saw Vicki hit the ground. Look! Look! Danger! Hurt!

Swan, still a man, shushed Dibs, and then sent him back to the cabin for clothes for Swan and something for Vicki to borrow.

"Go fast, Dibs. I'll start carrying her home, but we need the clothing before we leave the forest."

So Dibs ran. He ran very fast, a little scared that something bad had happened to Vicki. She was such a pretty lady, and so nice. He wanted her to be okay. He wanted her to make more brownies and lemonade and he wanted to feel her fingers in his fur.

He didn't want her to be scared and to think Swan and him had done bad things to her.

Dibs shifted when he got to the cabin, grabbing Swan's sweatpants and t-shirt, and then grabbing an old, oversized sweatshirt that had belonged to Swan, but was now his. He almost put it back again, but he wanted Vicki to have something from both of them and he really hoped he'd get it back later.

Pushing the clothes into a bag he could carry easily in wolf form, he shifted again, grabbed a strap and took off. He was so fast that Swan wasn't more than halfway back to Vicki's, still deep in the forest when he caught up with them.

"Good boy," praised Swan, fingers sinking briefly in his fur.

Swan put Vicki down so he could dress, and Dibs went over to her, scenting her and then licking her face. She moaned softly, moving restlessly. So scared. So tired. So lonely. He could smell it all over her.

"I need your help getting this on her, Dibs."

Dibs gave her one last lick, and then shifted, holding her up while Swan put the sweatshirt over her head and started feeding her arms into the sleeves.

"I gave her mine that used to be yours."

"Good choice," Swam smiled at him, but he could tell Swan was tense, unhappy.

"What's wrong with her, Swan? Why is she so scared?"

"Because, to her it's all strange and different. You and me, we've been werewolves our whole lives -- we never had to learn how to be like we are. When she was bitten, her whole world changed."

"Will she stop being scared?"

"I hope so." He got another sad smile from Swan, and then his big strong mate was picking Vicki up. "Hopefully she will come to accept us and what she has become."

"I'd like that! She's pretty. She's nice."

"Yes, she is."

Dibs shifted, bounding ahead of Swan and Vicki, and then coming back to them, circling them before heading back out. He only stopped when he reached the edge of the forest, looking over at Vicki's place. Uh-oh, the back door was broken, glass all over the floor from when Swan had pushed his way in last night. The pretty lady was maybe going to be mad.

He sat, waiting at the edge of the trees for Swan to catch up to him.

She was shaking -- he could see it -- and she was trying to change, her body wanting to be close and warm.

"Hurry," Swan called, running for the open door.

He bounded along with them, barking and yipping. They cleared the door, Swan cursing as he ran over the glass. She barked, flailing, caught in mid-shift. How could someone do this? Hurt her like this? Swan growled, the sound strange in his man form and Dibs whimpered, upset and wanting to comfort her.

Laying her on the ground in the front room, far away from the broken door, Swan talked to her quietly. "Shh. It's okay, Vicki. You're home, you're safe."

She relaxed, eyes blinking open, tongue slipping out, a rough sound escaping her.

Swan stayed a man and Dibs stayed as a wolf, both of them staying close. "One or the other," Swan told her. "Be either the wolf or the woman. With the moon not out, you should be able to control it with your will."

Those pretty, pretty eyes opened, stared at Swan, and then the fur faded back.

"There you go. You can control it." Swan was so calm. Dibs took a moment to admire him.

"What... did someone drug me?"

"No. It was the wolf bite. Do you remember me telling you about how it wasn't a regular wolf who bit you?"

Dibs barked -- they'd been through this already. She reached out for him, patting him without thought as she nodded. He yipped happily and licked her hand.

"Do you remember Dibs here turning from a human into a wolf?"

"I..." She curled up a little, that fear scent coming back.

Dibs whimpered and licked her cheek. He didn't want her to be afraid.

"We aren't going to hurt you, Vicki."

"This is crazy. I'm going crazy, aren't I?"

"No, it is very real." Swan petted her arm.

Dibs barked. Not crazy!

"I don't know what to do. My head hurts."

"You need to eat. And to sleep. The moon will pull you out again tonight. Dibs and I will run with you, help you."

He heard her stomach snarl, knew that she must be starving. He barked. He could go catch food!

Swan shook his head. "Shift back Dibs. She'll need to eat from her human stores."

He pouted, but did as he was told, shivering as his fur disappeared.

Vicki whimpered softly, staring at him. "I... I... Do you need clothes?"

Swan answered for him. "He can wear the sweat-shirt you're wearing now -- it is his. And you have your own clothes now that we're in your house, yes?"

He nodded, bouncing. His sweatshirt which smelled like Swan and him and her now.

"Yeah. Yeah..." She stood up, swaying. "I'll be right back."

Swan reached for her, steadying her. "Are you sure you want to go alone?"

"I... I don't know."

"We can go with you, make sure you don't fall."

Dibs nodded in agreement with Swan; Vicki didn't look very steady.

"I want to go home." Vicki looked at him, stared into his eyes. "Make it go away."

Dibs shook his head. "I can't make it go away. Nobody can."

Swan backed him up. "You have to deal with this, Vicki. And you are in your house."

"Why did you... Who bit you? Did I just ask that?"

Dibs looked to Swan. His mate could explain these things better than him. Swan was better at a lot of things. Except running. He was better at that.

"Many of us are born this way. Dibs and I were. Nobody bit us. But if one of our kind bites a human, it changes you."

"It can't be real, can it?"

One of Swan's eyebrows went up. "Would you like to see Dibs shift back to wolf form again?"

"No." She stepped away, shook her head. "No, I don't. I'm sorry, I don't."

Vicki led them further into the house, the walls covered in paintings, in photographs of wolves everywhere.

"You like wolves," Dibs noted, taking it all in, eyes wide.

Swan nodded. "Like you were meant to be bitten."

"I'm a painter. It's what I do." Her fingers traced her scar.

"Why wolves?" Swan asked as they came into a room with a large bed in it.

In this room there were huge paintings, hanging on wires from the ceiling. The moon.

"I don't know. I like their eyes."

Dibs looked at the paintings and then at Swan. He'd never seen anything like it.

"Are these new?" Swan asked, as mesmerized as he was by the huge canvases.

"Yes. These are. I'm working on others now." She turned her back, stripped the sweatshirt off, tugged on a huge, fluffy black robe.

Swan passed the sweatshirt over to him and he pulled it on. It had been big on Swan, on him it was huge, going down far enough to cover his vulnerable bits.

Vicki went to a bureau, started brushing her hair in harsh, rough strokes.

Dibs vibrated, hungry and tired. He wanted to eat and then curl up with Swan and Vicki, nap until the moon called to them again. "Food?" he asked plaintively. If they weren't going to eat Vicki's stores, he wanted to go out and hunt a rabbit or a chipmunk.

"I. Yeah. Yeah, I have oatmeal. I have eggs? Bacon?"

He perked up at the mention of eggs and bacon. He wanted meat. So did Vicki, even if she didn't know it yet.

Swan nodded, patting his arm. "Yes, eggs and bacon would be nice. Come to the kitchen with us -- we'll all make it together. You need to eat."

"O...okay. Okay." She moved slowly, almost like she was sick or dreaming. The fear, though, that was easing.

Dibs resisted the urge to give her a lick. Barely.

He followed as she and Swan headed over to the kitchen, the breeze from the back door bringing with it the scents of the forest that he recognized, even in human form. He wanted real food! Then milk and eggs, bacon and orange juice were pulled out, along with a little basket of muffins that smelled so sweet.

Oh. Good food.

He started to bounce in place, hovering over Vicki.

Swan swatted his ass. "Stay out of the way if you aren't going to help."

"You can have a muffin. I've been so hungry; I've been cooking like I'm feeding an army."

He snagged one, biting into it. Oh, she was a good cook. "'S good," he told her around a mouthful. She nodded, cooking quickly, quietly, everything smelling like heaven.

Dibs stood close to Swan, watching. "Smells so good." His stomach growled and he grinned, bouncing and rubbing against Swan's lean strength.

The bacon and eggs landed on the table, the plates clattering. "I'm going to bathe, before I eat. You two can have what you'd like."

Swan growled. "You need to eat. Take the plate

with you."

There were undercurrents he didn't understand and he whimpered, desperate to fall on the food, wanting the pack together.

Her eyes flashed, blood rising up through her body -- something very close to arousal. "Don't snap at me."

Swan's nostrils flared. "Please take a plate with you."

Dibs could hear her rumbling, hear her calling for them, to be touched. Licked. Tasted.

He shook his head. "No! No, don't go!" He reached out, fingers sliding on her cheeks, down along her neck. "Together." Couldn't Swan smell it?

"I. It'll get cold." At her words, Dibs reached out, stole a piece of bacon and ate it. Oh. Good. Almost as good as the idea of them, together.

Swan rolled his eyes. "Eat. All of us. Everything else can wait."

Dibs nodded, grabbing more bacon and holding it to her mouth. She opened for him, and he almost moaned. Pretty. So pretty. So soft... His fingers slipped into her mouth, rubbing the inside of her lips.

"Dibs..." He knew that warning tone in Swan's voice and, like he so often did, he ignored it.

She moaned and he could smell her. Smell her. He flashed a look at Swan, saw his mate's eyes glued to where his fingers met Vicki's mouth. Grinning, he took his fingers away and pressed his lips against hers instead. Her eyes went wide, her lips parting for him. He pressed his tongue inside, tasting her, feeling her warmth and breathing her breath.

She stepped backward, but Swan was there, behind her, solid and warm. Dibs took a quick kiss from Swan, and then returned to Vicki's mouth. She tasted so different, but good, so good.

"I..." Her nipples were hard; he could feel them against his chest.

His cock began to fill, and he whined, pushing harder into the kiss.

"Shh, easy Dibs. Gentle."

How could he be? She smelled so good, like heaven, like sex, like home. He reached for Swan, sliding his hand through the long hair, fingers massaging Swan's scalp. Swan could shh; he was kissing and feeling.

She was trembling, shivering, moaning into his lips. Dibs pushed against her, pushing her up against Swan. His mate moaned, head dipping, mouth sliding on Vicki's neck. He could smell her need, sweet and tart, and it made his mouth water. He slid open her robe, fingers moving on her belly. She was so soft, so good against his fingers.

She gasped, belly going tight and she stilled, eyes searching his. He smiled and licked her cheek, her lips. She tasted so good.

"I. This is probably..." Vicki swallowed, lips chasing his tongue. "A terrible idea."

"Oh, no! This is really good! Better than running!" He licked her cheek again and then pressed his tongue into her mouth, fingers sliding up her body. She was so different from Swan, but it was good.

Her laughter tasted like sunshine. Honestly. Truly.

He slid his free hand down Swan's arm, his other hand connecting with Vicki's breast. He gasped, the weight of it unfamiliar, but good. Swan's hand joined his, moving their fingers to the hard nipple, Swan tugging the bit of flesh. His eyes went wide, waiting to see if that hurt or felt good like it did when Swan touched him there.

Vicki's throat worked, the scent of hungry female more and more intense. Oh. Oh, yes. He beamed at Swan, his mate chuckling and bending to kiss him, trapping her between them as Swan's tongue swept through his mouth. Moaning, he opened wide to Swan and rubbed against Vicki. It was wonderful!

Her robe opened and they got more skin, more soft, warm flesh to touch.

Swan's lips left his in favor of sliding on Vicki's neck and Dibs whimpered and kissed her again, tongue licking inside her mouth. She tasted so good, even better like this than as the wolf. One cry after another pushed into his lips, her hips rolling. He humped against her, her skin so soft against his prick. Her curls tickled his cock, her belly was rounded and soft, so warm, so hot.

"Swan. Vicki. Swan." His eyes were huge, his heart beating hard in his chest. His prick slipped between her legs.

"I. This is..." She shuddered against him, fingers opening and closing.

"Good! It's good." He might not be smart like Swan, but he knew a good thing when he saw it. Felt it. Whatever.

Her soft chuckle made his cock throb. "I've never... not with two men, not with strangers."

"Not strangers! Dibs and Swan. Pack!" He knew that, too.

"Shh," whispered Swan. "Hush and just do it, you two."

"Pack?" At her words, Swan tweaked her nipple and she arched, bucking against him, his cock sliding against her wetness.

Dibs shot a look at Swan, turned on, but half-panicked.

"Do what comes naturally, Dibs. It'll make you both feel good."

So he slid his cock back and forth and she was slick and wet and he wanted in. Could he go in? Her body was soft, slick, warm and wet around him and she took him in easily. His eyes half rolled back into his head and he whimpered, hips sawing, pumping his cock in and out of her body.

Vicki moaned, rocking and shuddering for him, calling out in short, sharp barks. He trilled back at her, buried deep inside her. He barked again as he met her brilliant eyes. Oh, yes. Pack. Their pack. Her body rippled, the heat flooding her.

"Vicki..." He had no words.

And it only got better when Swan leaned in and wrapped his lips around Vicki's skin, pulling up a mark. A flush climbed up Vicki's body, her orgasm sweet, echoing inside him. Theirs. She had to be theirs. Whining happily, he kept moving, his balls drawing up. The pleasure rose up sharply and he came, yipping as he filled her.

They stumbled into the big room with the soft couches, the three of them settling down on one. He curled up with them, one hunger satisfied, the other could wait until they'd napped.

Chapter Six

She woke up between two men.

Two.

Two men.

Two men, one of which didn't seem totally sane, and the other who was too innocent to be real.

Two men.

Oh, God.

She slid off the sofa on shaky legs. Dusk was falling, the moon beginning to appear in the sky.

Two men.

Two naked men.

She'd lost her mind.

Dibs whimpered softly, Swan patting him, soothing him back to sleep. Dark grey eyes looked at her, though, Swan standing as well.

"The moon is coming," he said softly. "You'll run with us again tonight."

"Do you know how insane this all sounds? It's like I slid down the rabbit hole." She closed her robe, eyes drawn to the moon again.

"You've seen it with your own eyes and surely you remember shifting last night, running with us." Swan took her chin in his hands and turned her to face the window. "I know you feel her call."

"But why? Why bite me? I wasn't hurting anyone..." She moaned, swaying a bit, her nerves buzzing.

"I don't know why, Vicki." There was a tone in Swan's voice when he said her name. Something that made her shiver deep inside. "Any laws we are governed by are unwritten, but the most strongly held to is that if you do bring someone over, you must teach them what they need to know."

"I need to go take a shower. I'm aching inside." Aching, hungry, aroused.

He shook his head. "There won't be time." Even as he said it, Dibs stirred on the sofa, body changing as he woke.

She stepped closer to Swan, shivering in something she didn't understand. Swan's arms came around her. He was so warm and she felt better somehow when he held her, like she was protected in his arms.

Dibs, the wolf, came and rubbed against their legs, tongue lolling as he looked up at them. Then he barked sharply, twice, and padded toward the back door. Swan walked them to the door, hands smoothing her robe away, baring her for the touch of the moon.

"Don't be afraid of it," Swan whispered, breath teasing her skin. "Revel in it."

"I'm trying. I don't understand all this." Her mind didn't, but her body seemed to, tense muscles trying to relax.

"You don't have to understand. Your body knows -- just trust your instincts." Swan raised his head, sniffing hard. "Tonight we will hunt." Dibs came running back, barking and barking at them. Listen, he's berating us, telling us to come run with him."

"He... he's..." She shuddered, a sob escaping her. "It burns."

"That's because you're fighting it. Don't fight it Vicki. Flow into it -- just let it happen."

Vicki stretched, trying to ease the ache, her body sliding against Swan's. They both crouched, his arms surrounding her as her world slid from underneath her.

And then he was rubbing against her, growling softly. It was comforting, arousing. The moon called, demanded she run. She rumbled, muzzle sliding against his before she headed out into the woods, greeting Dibs with a bark. Dibs barked back, so happy. He came running to her, rubbing their muzzles together and growling playfully. And then he took off.

She gave chase, running through the trees like she was meant to. She could hear Swan behind her, powerful muscles bringing him quickly up to her. He barked as they ran, the sound joyous. The males flanked her, protecting her, guiding her through the leaves.

Dibs barked suddenly, nose up, and Swan encouraged her to do the same.

Food!

She bared her teeth, hunger so desperate it hurt.

Swan barked an order at Dibs, who took off toward the right while she and Swan continued forward. Her nose was on the ground, following the scent, her stomach leading her. Swan's low growl warned her a moment before the rabbit shot across their path, flushed out by a noisy, eager Dibs.

She leapt, jaws snapping around its throat, blood flooding her mouth.

She heard Swan's bark of praise, and then Dibs barked, too, trying to push her away from her kill. Snarling, she pushed back, threatened. Dibs barked, the sound sharp, and he tossed his head toward Swan who was waiting, teeth bared slightly.

She backed away, ears flat, instincts battering her from all sides.

Dibs licked her muzzle, cleaning her while Swan moved in on her rabbit -- her rabbit! -- and tore it open. Swan ate the heart and stomach, and then backed away. Dibs pounced the meat, quicker than her. Snarling, she turned, running deeper into the woods, away from the others. She let her instincts take her, flushing out a mouse and snapping it down. Swan's bark was proud and he encouraged her to find more food, the three of them making a meal of the small beasts in the forest.

She snarled whenever they came too near, protecting her take. Dibs would make her back off now and then, and let Swan have the heart. By the end of the hunt, she was confused, frustrated, and she turned, loping back to her den. Dibs followed, trying to head her off, deeper into the forest.

Running in circles, she felt her confusion growing as she fought her instincts. Swan barked hard, stopping them both in their tracks. She stared, panting, whining in sheer frustration. Swan nipped her heels, heading her into the forest. His growl was sure, insistent.

She snapped back, growling low. He didn't back down, though, insisting she go where he and Dibs wanted. She ran and then fought, then ran. Everything within her seemed to be spinning, confused. Finally the large male jumped her, mouth on her throat and she relaxed, panting, eyes rolling as the storm within her calmed.

Settled, she let him lead her and before long they reached the cabin from the night before. Dibs bounded up and pushed the door open. It smelled like them. It smelled safe. She headed in, sniffing hard. Oh. Bedding. Soft. She leapt up, turning in circles.

Dibs barked and bounded up after her. The young wolf made room for Swan though, yipping softly.

She rested her chin on her paws, curling in tight. Tired.

She was so tired.

The males wrapped around her, and they were all warm and cozy, Dibs going to sleep just like that. She stared at the alpha, blinking slower and slower. He licked her muzzle and then put his nose on his own paws, his low growl comforting.

She sighed, eyes closing as she fell into sleep.

Chapter Seven

Swan woke up before the others and made a quick inspection of the forest around the cabin, making sure everything was as it should be and that there were no strange scents. Satisfied, he returned to the cabin, bumping the door closed with his hind end.

Dibs and Vicki were curled together, sharing body heat. It was good. The more time Vicki spent with them, the more comfortable she'd be. Eventually she'd realize she belonged with them, that she was Pack.

The wolf part of her already knew, for the most part. The human, though... Swan sighed and climbed into the nest of covers, settling close and watching, wondering how soon after she woke Vicki would take on her human form.

She hummed, pushing back against him, rocking idly. Oh, yes, the wolf part of her knew.

He gave a low growl, mouth open on her neck, letting her feel his teeth. Letting her feel her Alpha. Her eyes opened, her tail thumping for him as she began to wake up. He licked her muzzle, thumped his own tail in return. She was a beautiful lady; she was even more beautiful as a wolf than she was as a human.

She lapped at his chin, chuffing softly. Pack. Yes. His Pack. Dibs whimpered and moved, no doubt smelling them. Swan gave him a lick to soothe him. Vicki stretched, sighing softly. She would change soon, he could tell. The wolf was so foreign to her. He rubbed against her, licked her muzzle again, hoping that when she changed this time, she wouldn't be so freaked out.

She whimpered softly, muscles rippling. It didn't hurt them to change, but she was so new, so foreign to it, that it seemed to.

He shifted as well, hands sliding over her skin to ease her. "It's okay," he murmured. "You're safe."

She nodded, eyes closing. "I had the weirdest dreams."

Still not believing it to be real yet. He managed not to sigh, that wouldn't help anything. "Did you?" he asked instead. Perhaps she had dreamed while she slept.

"Mmmhmm. I dreamed about when I was a little girl. I was lost in the woods."

"And did a wolf save you and lead you home?"

"I don't... I slept in a cave until my father found me."

"Did it really happen or was it just a dream?" Lost in the woods, sleeping in caves. If it had happened, perhaps there was a part of her that had called to the wolf to bite her. Not that that excused his leaving her to her own devices, but it would explain the biting.

"I got lost. They say there's no way I remember it right, though." She sighed, fingers sliding through Dibs' fur. "I must have imagined it."

Dibs stretched beneath her touch, and yawned.

"No, I believe you." Maybe she'd been drawn to them, to the wolves. "It would explain your paintings, your fascination with wolves."

"Maybe. Maybe. This all seems like a fantasy, somehow. Like I watched the wolves so long that I became one."

"It's real, though," he whispered in her ear as Dibs stretched, body shifting and elongating until Dibs was a man.

Her nipples went tight, her legs shifting. "Oh."

He smiled as he smelled her arousal, his own making itself know, his prick hardening.

Dibs' eyes went wide, and then he grinned, leaning in to lick first his, and then Vicki's cheeks.

"I. Good morning. Is... I'm naked."

"We're all naked. It's what happens after a night of running with the wolves."

Dibs nodded. "Naked is good. Makes it easier to love."

"I've never made love to two men together. Never." She didn't smell unwilling, not at all.

"Yes you did!" Dibs laughed. "Yesterday!"

Swan chuckled. "We are a pair. Now a trio..."

"A trio." Her eyes looked stunned, but she shifted closer. "We don't know each other yet..."

"We do! I'm Dibs and that is Swan and you are Vicki!"

"We are pack," Swan expanded. That was all that mattered.

"You say that like it answers everything."

"For us, it does. You will come to understand that soon." When she accepted what was happening was real.

"I don't..."

Dibs interrupted her, hands sliding up her belly to cup her breasts, almost like Dibs was offering them to him.

"Mmm... good, Dibs." He slid his arm around her, fingers teasing her nipples. They went hard, tight, and he couldn't help his growl.

He rubbed his need against her ass, and watched Dibs do the same against her belly. Bending, Dibs took her left nipple into his mouth, licking it and Swan's fingers both.

"Oh!" Her ass bucked, rolled against him, her fingers tangling in Dibs' hair.

"You are beautiful. And sexy, Vicki. We will both love you."

Dibs moaned happily around her nipple.

"I. This is over my head." No. No, he didn't think

so. He thought this was exactly what she needed.

"Stop thinking," he ordered. She needed to trust her instincts more and her brain less.

Dibs kept sucking and he leaned in to kiss a line along her jaw, tongue flicking at the corner of her lips.

"Kiss me?" She was so lovely, vulnerable. Needy. Hungry.

"Yes." Swan turned her head slightly, lips closing over hers. She tasted so different from Dibs, and yet already he tasted that she was his, that she was Pack.

She opened to him, tongue sliding against his, eyelashes brushing his skin. He rubbed harder against her as her arousal, and his, spiked. Dibs groaned, humping against her belly. It rocked her back against him, making him groan.

One of her legs slid up along Dibs' thighs, Dibs' hand tugging it higher. His prick slid between her legs, nudging against her. Groaning, he shifted, pulling her up and back, the tip of his cock slipping inside her. Hot. Wet. Slick. He pulled harder, hips rolling as she took him in.

Dibs was still working her nipples, sucking on one and then the other, hands stroking and hefting her breasts. Swan felt like howling, the scent of the three of them hot, exciting. Her hair surrounded them -- filling his nostrils with the smell of rain and sex and woman.

Whimpering, Dibs pushed harder, hips sliding his prick along Vicki's belly. The movements brought him and Vicki together faster, his thrusts growing stronger. Growling a little, he bit at her neck, teeth finding skin.

"Oh. Oh, damn." He felt that all within her, muscles squeezing and trembling.

Dibs came first, head going back on a howl, the

scent of his pleasure sudden and strong. Vicki shook for them, riding his prick, body surrounding him like a glove. He pushed into her over and over, long strokes, working to share pleasure with her.

He took Dibs' hand, brought it down to slide through her curls, showing him the hub of nerves guaranteed to drive her wild. Dibs was always a quick learner, and this was no different. Soon Vicki was writhing between them, her walls squeezing him rhythmically

Her cries were wild, sharp, calling to them and driving them both crazy. His hips snapped, howls leaving him, mixing with Dibs'. With one last howl, he came, filling her with his seed.

They rested together, the three of them panting, bodies coming to rest. Dibs kissed Vicki and then him, looking like he was going to bound up and run.

"Shh. Nap." He made it an order and Dibs whimpered once, licked his face and settled, cuddling in.

He had his Pack in his arms. Two now.

His.

Chapter Eight

They napped. And then they went back to Vicki's house with the windows. Vicki hadn't changed and Swan stayed a man with her, leaving Dibs to run circles around them, going ahead and coming back, barking, encouraging them to go faster. Dibs didn't understand why Vicki didn't want to run.

Then he and Swan fixed the door, hammering a piece of wood over the frame.

"What's this 'shower' we're here for, Swan?" Dibs asked. Vicki had seemed very excited about.

"Like in the river, only the water pours down over you."

"Oh." Dibs wasn't very sure about that at all. The river water was cold, even in the summer, and he wasn't so sure about standing in it in his human form.

Swan chuckled. "Go on. Vicki said she'd get it ready. I'll be there in a minute."

Dibs pounced. Swan and kissed him, and then followed the sound of water. There was fog pouring from the thing, Vicki standing under running water, hands sliding over her body. It looked like she was enjoying herself. And the fog... it was very strange.

Dibs resisted the urge to shift back to the wolf where at least his fur would keep him warm. He reached out, gasping and snatching his hand back when the water was hot. Hot.

Green-green eyes stared at him. "You okay?"

"The water is hot!" He reached out and touched it again. Not cold!

"Yeah. You want me to turn it down? I can."

"No..." Eyes wide, he stepped cautiously into the shower stall, gasping again as the hot water poured down over him.

"Mmm. Feels good, huh?" She grabbed a bar of

soap, started rubbing it over her skin.

"It's hot!" He laughed, lifting his face to the falling water.

"I like my showers nice and warm." She stretched up, reaching for the water.

He moved so it flowed over her and he reached out, fingers sliding over her slick skin.

"Mmm." She moaned, looking at him. "I like that."

He beamed at her and kept touching, fascinated by the hot water coming down and the slickness of her skin.

A low chuckle from the doorway caught his attention and he called to Swan. "You have to come! Hot -- the water is hot!"

"I know. It's good, isn't it?"

Dibs nodded eagerly. It was wonderful!

"There's room. I have a huge shower." He thought that Vicki's smile was like magic.

Swan joined them and Dibs bounced. "Isn't it wonderful?"

"It is." Swan raised his face to the spray just like Dibs had.

Laughing, Dibs slid his hands on Swan to see if the water had the same effect on Swan's skin as it did on Vicki's. Slick, warm -- Swan felt so good. Not as slick and smooth as Vicki, but so good.

Curious, he bent to taste Vicki. The soap was sharp, flowery, odd, but underneath it was Vicki, it was their Pack. He hummed licking harder trying to clean the soapy scents from her. She moaned a little, nipples going hard and tight.

They called to him and he sucked one into his mouth, pulling on it, the taste of soap fading as he swirled his tongue around it. She tasted so good -- her -- not the soap. Her.

"Oh." Swan's arms came around her, held her

up. Held her up for him.

He grinned up at his mate and bit down gently, making Vicki jerk between them.

Swan held her breast for him, thumb pushing into his mouth along with Vicki's nipple. Groaning, Dibs sucked hard on both.

Oh. Oh, look at how she needed them. Her hips rocked and bucked and her head was thrown back as she cried. His prick pushed against her belly as his hips rocked to meet hers. He knew that Swan's cock was hard, heavy against her lower back.

He let go of her nipple and kissed her lips, tongue pushing into her mouth before he broke the kiss again. "Can we both have you?" he asked. "Together?"

"I... I have a bed..." Her cheeks were pink, flushed, eyes wide.

That was a yes, wasn't it?

His eyes flashed to Swan who nodded, who grinned.

Laughing, Dibs bounced out of the shower, shaking the water from his skin.

"There are towels!" She was laughing, the sound merry, joyous.

"Towels?" He looked at Swan, who was also laughing at him. His mate threw a soft, fluffy rectangle at him.

"Soft!"

They were huge and soft and bright red and just wonderful. Vicki wrapped one around her body, one around that beautiful mass of hair. Swan wrapped one around his body, too, and so Dibs did the same, laughing. "Why don't we have towels, Swan?"

"Because when we do bathe, it's in the river as wolves, Dibs."

"Oh. Right." He bounced over to Vicki and licked her face. "Thank you!"

"You are the lickingest thing." She winked, leading them down the hall to the room with the huge paintings of the moon, of wolves.

"Licking is good! Isn't it, Swan?"

"Kissing is better for humans, Dibs."

"I can kiss!"

He jumped onto the bed, laughing up at the giant painting of the moon over the bed as he bounced. "We need a bed, Swan!" They're nest of pillows and covers was good, but this was better. The bedding smelled of woman, of Vicki, the entire room seductive, arousing. He rubbed himself against the sheets, adding his own scent there. Then he lay back and opened his arms. He wanted his mates.

Vicki dried her hair off, stepping closer. "You're a very interesting man."

"That's a good thing, right?"

"Yes. Yes, it's a good thing." Her chuckle settled right in his balls, made him feel so fine.

Dibs wanted her. He lay back and stroked his cock, doing what felt good. "Come and have me."

Her towel fell and she slid into the sheets, cuddling into his arms. He wrapped his arms around her and kissed her, loving the way she tasted in his mouth. She already tasted like Pack. Swan came onto the bed as well and Dibs was perfectly happy. The bed was big enough for all of them, big enough and warm. Vicki's hands were on him, on Swan, the thin fingers trembling.

"Do you have anything slick, Vicki?" Swan asked.

"I... I have baby oil. I use it in the winters for my skin." She stretched up, found a tiny bottle that she handed to Swan.

Swan took the bottle from her and stroked her cheek. "You are sure this is okay?"

Dibs waited eagerly for her answer.

"Will you make it good?" The words were almost too soft to hear.

Dibs nodded. "Swan always makes it wonderful!"

Swan chuckled and rubbed his head. "Thank you, pup. And yes, I will make it good. We want to take pleasure with you, Vicki."

"I haven't... I mean, I. Somebody kiss me."

Swan got there before he did, so Dibs watched as Swan's tongue swept into her mouth. So lovely, it made him whimper. Vicki's body relaxed, seemed to melt, her curves petted and molded in Swan's hands. He knew how she felt, Swan's hands were wonderful. So were his kisses and his rutting.

Dibs whimpered and Swan broke the kiss. "Ride him, lovely lady, and I will have you, too."

She turned to him, trembling, and he needed to touch her, relax her. His fingers slid over her shoulders and stroked down along her back. She was so very soft. Dibs leaned up and touched his lips to hers, tongue licking quickly into her mouth.

Swan's hands joined his, rubbing her in long, slow strokes, until she starting moving with them. He could feel her growing wet as she rubbed against his thigh and he moved her so she straddled him, pushing his cock between her legs.

He fit perfectly, sinking inside her, held in that perfect, heated, wet place.

His hands slid to her hips, lifting her and bringing her down as he bucked up into here. "Oh! Oh, Vicki, so good!" Her pretty eyes went all heavy-lidded, lips swollen and parted. So pretty. "Oh, Swan! You have to feel!"

Swan chuckled. "Next time, Dibs. I am back here today."

He couldn't see what Swan was doing, but he felt it in the way her walls closed around him, almost rippling. Vicki moaned, movement slowing as Swan touched her. He slid his hands around her bottom, feeling for where Swan's fingers pushed into her.

She was trembling for them, but she still moved, sliding between his cock and Swan's fingers. He leaned up, licking at her nipples, and then taking one into his mouth, sucking it. He felt that around his cock, too, felt the way her whole body shook. It made him want to come, but he concentrated on making her feel good instead, so he would still be hard when Swan was inside her, too.

"H...harder, Dibs. Please." His eyes rolled as she groaned for him.

"This?" he asked, pushing into her. "Or this?" He took her other nipple into his mouth, pulling hard on it.

"Yes!" Her cry was echoed by Swan's chuckle, low and aroused.

"Slow for a moment, Dibs, and then we'll be inside Vicki together."

Oh, oh, he could go slow; he could wait. For that he could.

Vicki's body seemed to tighten around him as Swan's face appeared over her pale, smooth shoulder. He reached up to touch Swan's cheek, and then Vicki's, his breath coming in short, sharp pants. "Mated," he murmured. "All three."

"I. So full..." Vicki licked his palm, lips open, eyes wide.

He beamed at her. "Licking!" Then he leaned up and licked her lips.

Swan laughed. "Dibs. Slowly. We move together."

His eyes widened and he nodded, licking Vicki again, hips moving with Swan's motions.

"I... Oh." Vicki leaned hard against him, belly slick with her sweat.

Swan followed her down, and Dibs reached, petting both of them, the sensations and smells and tastes all wrapping up together and making him dizzy. He whimpered, body bucking, pushing his cock deep inside her.

"Kiss me. Dibs. Baby. Come on." Her lips fastened onto his as they started moving, all of them. Together.

His tongue pushed into her mouth, fucking her lips. Groaning, he grabbed her head and pushed his tongue deeper. Oh, oh. This was better than running, better because they were moving as one. He could feel Swan's cock, moving so close to his, both of them making this beautiful woman theirs. He wrapped one hand around Vicki's hip, the other slid to cover Swan's, their fingers twisting together. Together like the three of them.

Vicki's breath was coming faster, the gasps sharp, almost growls. The heat around him was nearly unbearable, the pressure so sweet.

He began to howl, the sound forced out of him. The sound made Vicki shudder and Dibs saw Swan lean down, teeth on one of her shoulders, marking her. He howled again, hips thrusting hard, pushing deep inside her as he came, marking her within.

Vicki sobbed, hips jerking, gasping into his lips. He held on and kissed, Swan's thrusts moving him and Vicki, pushing them together. She shuddered from top to bottom, eyes wide, almost scared, like it was so big she couldn't cope.

He stroked her arms and licked her right cheek. "It's good, Vicki."

"I... It's big." She pressed her cheek against his, rubbing hard.

"He feels wonderful, doesn't he?" He beamed past her at Swan, his mate smiling back at him.

"Mmm." She grabbed his hand, drew it down

to the place where they were joined. "Touch me, hmm?"

He slid his fingers, gasping as she moaned and bucked. He found the little nub and rubbed it with two fingers, sliding over it.

"Oh." Whatever that did made Swan growl, jerk, buck above her.

He all but bounced, fingers rubbing, tapping at her. Vicki's head fell over, chest heaving, body shifting and sliding on his half-hard cock.

"Don't stop," Swan ordered and Dibs nodded, kept touching Vicki. Swan groaned, moving faster, rocking Vicki against him.

Her cries vibrated against his skin, his cock filling again, from the pressure and pleasure all around him. He started moving again, the three of them flowing together. Vicki started moaning, fluttering around him, cries steady and needy and constant.

He couldn't believe how good it felt, to be three like this. He whimpered softly, and Swan called back to him. Vicki moaned, fingers dragging up along his side. His own fingers stayed between them, working that little spot that made her gasp and moan and ripple.

Swan's eyes met his, shining, bright, hungry.

Happy.

Whole.

He tilted his head back and howled, hips jerking, pushing himself into Vicki. The sound was strange in his man throat, but still good. Swan's sound matched his, making the room ring. Vicki's cry harmonized, joining with theirs and making the sound something new.

"Now," cried out Swan and Dibs followed that command, coming again.

They all slumped together, Vicki quiet, eyes closed, lips swollen and so pretty. He petted her and then Swan, and then her again. "This is good."

Swan leaned to kiss him. "This is ours. Our pack. We'll protect her, love her."

"Yes. Mates. Three now." He would protect his pack. Vicki and Swan.

Chapter Eight

She could hear voices downstairs and she tried to drown them out, throwing herself into her work, trying to paint, trying to work out the mingled emotions and needs inside her. Trying to find her way out of the rabbit hole.

It was getting dark, so she brushed her hair out of her face, heading to flip the lights on. She really should eat something. Really.

Dibs came bounding up the steps, smiling widely at her. "Vicki! The moon has come!"

"Has it?" It looked like she was going to stay in her own body, nice and human. "Cool."

Dibs nodded. "It's time to run! Come on!"

"What? I... It's only at the full moon, Dibs." She needed to answer emails, cook supper, pay some bills.

He laughed and shook his head. "No! No, come and run!" He licked her cheek and grabbed her hand. "Come on!"

She stumbled with him down the stairs, bumping against his arm. "Swan? What's he talking about?"

"Good evening, Vicki. Dibs would like to go for a run and he wants you to go along."

Dibs bounced and nodded beside her.

"But the moon's not full." She headed for the kitchen, needing something to drink.

The men followed her, Dibs in his characteristically enthusiastic bouncing, Swan at a more sedate place. "It doesn't have to be."

She grabbed the pitcher of tea. "I don't... It only happens when the moon's full, I think. I would remember."

"You can make it happen whenever you want" She could see Dibs roll his eyes as Swan spoke.

"No, I can't. I don't know how. Do you two want

tea?"

"No! I want to run! With you and Swan!" Dibs took her hand again and tugged her toward the back.

"You can change any time you want, Vicki. I can show you how, if you like."

"I..." Swan seemed so solid, so sure, where Dibs could unnerve her. "I could try, I guess."

"Woo!" Dibs laughed and bounced and licked her face.

Chuckling, Swan followed, too. "First things first. Clothes are a messy business and you're better off without them before changing."

"I've been naked more in the last few days... It's bizarre."

Dibs shook his head. "No! Wearing clothes is weird. Being natural is... being natural."

"People just can't go around... I'd get cold."

"Be the wolf! The wolf is warm!" Dibs laughed and shifted right before her eyes, becoming a wolf.

"I... I'm not a wolf." Was she?

Dibs barked, the sound unhappy.

Swan sighed, fingers stroking over her arms. "Vicki... you're a shifter. Like Dibs and I."

She found herself leaning into the touch. "It's just so hard to understand."

Dibs rubbed against her, and then got distracted by his tail. He began to chase it. Swan, though, was calm and strong, tugging her against him. "I know. It is easier if you don't think about it -- if you just let it happen."

Vicki let herself touch, hand sliding over Swan's ribs, counting each one. So strong. "You have such a gentle touch."

"Thank you." Her eyes closed, cheek on Swan's shoulder as her fingers moved to Swan's stomach.

He made a soft noise that was almost a growl,

muscles moving beneath her fingertips.

"Mmm." It got easier to melt into Swan's warmth, let all her worries go.

His arms went around her, pulling her close. "Maybe instead of what we usually do, we can do what you usually do in the evenings."

"I cook supper. Take long bubble baths." One hand rubbed down her back, made her arch as a pocket of tension let loose. "Oh..." Oh, she was so sore and that felt so good.

He brought both hands to the spot, rubbing. "Dibs will splash in your bath," Swan told her, chuckling.

"He's enthusiastic." And dear and he made her feel irresistible. Swan made her feel sensual.

"He loves life and he has no filters. We have never needed them."

As if Dibs knew they were talking about him, he shifted again, coming over. "Not running?" he asked sadly.

She sighed a little, pulled away from Swan. This wasn't her world. Not really. She lived at the edge of things. "Why don't you two go? I have work to do, supper to invent."

Swan didn't let her go, though, and he shook his head. "No. No running. Tonight we will do things that you usually do. Dibs just doesn't know anything else."

"I do!" protested Dibs. "But running is the best. Almost the best."

"Tell us how to help you invent supper, Vicki. We'll even put on clothes."

"Well, I think we could have pasta. Do you like that?" She'd fucked them both and she knew nothing about them.

"What's pasta?" Dibs asked.

Swan gave her an apologetic look. "We're pretty much meat eaters..."

"I..." She reached up, hugged Swan. "You two go run. Come back when you're done, huh? There will be food." This just was... insane.

"But how will we learn your ways if we go?"

"Everything can't change overnight and I'm feeling like I don't belong anywhere right now." Maybe like she was just going to cry.

"You belong with us." Dibs said it like it was obvious.

Swan nodded. "You do. And we want to make you feel like you belong."

She did start to cry then, just because they were so honest, so dear and she was such a fuck up.

"Don't cry!" Dibs licked at her cheeks, licking the tears away.

Swan was patting her. "We're not making you cry, are we? Please, we just want to make you happy."

"I'm just... it's so new and you're both dear and I'm..." She scrubbed at her cheeks. "I want to feel normal, whatever that is."

Dibs licked her face again, lapping at the tears.

"If we go it will never feel normal," Swan murmured.

"We..." She looked at Dibs, smiled. "You might like pasta. I know you'll like marble cake." She would meet them halfway and try as hard as they did.

"Cake? Is that like the cookies and lemonade?"

Swan laughed. "Dibs will like lots of food, if he's given a chance to taste it, I think. Now tell us what to do."

"Come on into the kitchen. We'll all figure it together."

Chapter Nine

Supper had been good. He and Dibs had 'helped' make it, though Swan was pretty sure they'd made it take much longer than if Vicki had been cooking by herself. She hadn't complained, though. Having just finished their cake, they were now on the couch, listening to pretty music. Well, he and Vickie were, Dibs was 'dancing'.

Vicki was drawing Dibs, him, pencil scratching on a thick pad of paper. Dibs came over and licked him and then Vicki, laughing, and then went back to bouncing around the room. Swan laughed and peeked at Vicki's papers. She made them look magical -- Dibs' eyes were lit up, his Dibs was beautiful -- strong, happy, wild.

"Is that how you see him?" She truly did belong with them.

"It's how he is." He was there, too. The Alpha. Looking like his father had when he was young.

"I like how you see us. We are Pack, we are beautiful to each other."

She nodded, legs curling up under herself, the action leaning her more fully against him. He hummed softly, enjoying her peaceful presence. So different than Dibs, already so dear.

Speaking of Dibs, his young mate finally finished his so-called dancing. Dibs threw himself down at their feet, leaning against the couch and laughing.

"You like that music, huh?" Vicki reached down, petted Dibs' hair.

Dibs nuzzled into her touches. "Yes."

"Good. I do, too."

Dibs bounced up and kissed her, and then gave him one, too, tongue sweeping through his mouth for a second. Her laughter seemed to dance around them both. It made Dibs laugh, too, and he climbed

133

up onto the couch, stretching out over both of them.

Vicki chuckled, tapped Dibs gently with the eraser bit of her pencil. "How do you two survive? I mean, how do you handle supplies, taxes, land?"

"Huh?" Dibs looked utterly confused.

Swan chuckled. "We own the land around the cabin and there is a firm that takes care of the money matters. We eat what we catch."

"Ah. I have gallery shows. I have one in Chicago in two weeks."

"Chicago? You're going away?"

Dibs sat up. "No! You can't go away!"

"I have to. I'll be gone for ten days. I have to be at the show; otherwise I can't pay my bills."

"When do you get back?" She needed to be home for the full moon. She would be trapped in a big city.

"Before the moon. I told them I had another appointment. It's not a big deal, trust me." She didn't sound sure of that, though. He could smell her worry, her fear, how she didn't want to leave their territory.

The Alpha in him wanted to order her not to go or go with her, protect her. He didn't know that he could, though. Dibs certainly wouldn't survive the big city. "Could someone do it for you?"

"Do what? Go? I'm the artist..."

Dibs was almost trembling. "I don't want you to go, Vickie. You belong here. With us."

"Shh. Shh, now. Don't stress." She reached for Dibs, comforting him, and Dibs started rubbing against her, scenting her.

He stroked her arm. "Does it have to be ten days?" It was such a long time to be without her, without any contact.

"I..." She leaned toward his touch, skin warming, her instincts coming to the fore, needing to be touched, groomed.

"Go, set things up, say hello and come back where you belong." Her skin was so beautiful and soft.

"The traveling is... Mmm." Her eyelids got heavy, the scent of pleasure strong. "That feels good."

"It would be better naked!" Dibs had already stripped before he started dancing.

Swan laughed at Dibs. His lover always got straight to the point.

Vicki chuckled. "I'd be cold."

"Dibs and I will keep you warm." He tilted her chin, taking a soft kiss. It warmed him all through.

She smiled, leaning into his kiss, fingers soft and gentle in his hair. He hummed as he kept the kiss going, tongue sweeping slowly through her mouth. He could feel Dibs working to keep from pouncing them, his mate all but vibrating against them.

Vicki's hair tumbled over his fingers, so soft, almost addictive. It wasn't at all like fur, and he stroked through it, spreading it out over her back. His name was whispered against his lips, so quiet, so happy. He looked into her eyes, wanting her to see his pleasure and joy. Oh, her cheeks flushed, her scent warming, becoming richer, deeper.

Dibs whimpered and Swan slid his free hand over his mate, finding and stroking Dibs' belly. Vicki's hand was there too, touching Dibs. He smiled at her as Dibs' whimpers turned into happy moans. Vicki relaxed, cheek against the sofa back, heart pounding.

Dibs whimpered again, the sound happy this time, his mate rubbing and arching against them. It wasn't rushed or hurried yet, but the smell of arousal was definitely on the air.

"Have you ever... I mean, are there many of you?

Us? I mean, around."

"We are territorial. The one that turned you --
he was in our territory with his pack at the end of
spring. We didn't talk to them, only signaled that
they should move on, and after a day or two, they
did. Several other packs have crossed our territory
in the last twenty years or so."

"I didn't bother you? Being here?"

"Only when you ventured into the woods last
month. Then we knew you were here and we had
to find you. Your scent was... " He twisted his lips,
trying to come up with the right word.

"Good," said Dibs. "You smell good -- human or
wolf."

"My perfume?" Swan knew she knew better,
knew that she could smell them, that their scent
eased her.

"No! You!" Dibs tugged her blouse up and nuzzled the skin of her belly. "You. You. You."

Swan rubbed Dibs' stomach some more. "Yes.
We don't like perfume." He wrinkled his nose.

"No? I used to. I threw it away after..." Her fingers brushed her scarred arm.

He wasn't surprised to hear that. His fingers followed hers, the texture of the scars interesting. "You
don't like it now either. It covers too much and your
nose is more sensitive now."

"No, I don't like it now. So much is changing."
Her skin goosepimpled up and she leaned in toward
him.

"For the better," he told her, nibbling on her lips
as Dibs continued to nuzzle her belly.

"Mmmhmm." He leaned her back a bit, drinking
from her lips, tongue sliding in to taste her.

Dibs' hands started to get busy, tugging at his t-
shirt and pulling it up out of his sweatpants, fingers
sliding up to find one of his nipples. He stopped that

hand and broke the kiss long enough to chide gently, "Slow down, pup, we have all night."

Vicki smiled, fingers tracing his eyebrows. "That sounds decadent. All night."

"We all have nowhere to be. Even the moon's call has lessened." Even Dibs didn't argue the point.

"Tomorrow, you'll have to show me how to change, so we can run with Dibs." Oh. Oh, she was theirs. She was trying so hard.

"Yes! Run!" Dibs laughed and blew against her belly.

Swan beamed at her.

Her laughter rang out, one leg wrapping around Dibs. Dibs laughed, too, tickling and licking. Swan chuckled, joining the play, fingers finding her ribs. Their laughter swelled, joined, all of them touching and tickling.

Swan settled back against the couch, his fingers no longer ticking, just caressing. She stretched for him, for both of them, letting them touch and see. He and Dibs both worked her blouse up over her head, Dibs petting her hair, and then her breasts, making a soft noise.

Swan traced her face, fingers coming back again and again to her lips. Her curves were lush, breasts and lips full and luscious. He thought he might be fascinated. He and Dibs both leaned in to take a nipple into their mouths at the same time. Dibs laughed and licked him, and then went back to Vicki's breast, as did he.

"I... I have two guys. Two. You can share."

Dibs laughed again, and latched onto the other nipple, grinning at him around it. He rolled his eyes at Dibs and bent to take the first nipple in his mouth. Her fingers tangled in his hair, her cry ringing out, almost surprised. He and Dibs both sucked, Dibs' fingers sliding on him, finding one of his nipples and tugging.

It was meditative, pulling and humming, tasting her, feeling her flesh, tight between his lips. Dibs was making noises, twisting and bucking, trying to hump against him. He took pity on the pup, free hand sliding to wrap his fingers around Dibs' cock. Dibs burned against his palm, fingers tightening as they moved.

Dibs' fingers slid down his chest and over his belly, searching beneath his waistband. He was hard, aching, needing to mark his pack, his lovers. Dibs' fingers seemed almost cool against his cock as they explored, index finger pushing against his slit, making him groan and jerk.

He left Vickie's nipple, moving up to lick his way into her lips. She looked debauched, lips parted, tongue flicking out to meet his. He took kiss after kiss, his hand working Dibs' prick, following the rhythm Dibs set on his cock.

She started shifting, sliding against him, lips clinging to his. Dibs tugged at her skirt, pulling it up and burying his face between her legs. Her eyes went wide for a second, and then a deep, raw moan pushed into his lips. He squeezed Dibs' cock in encouragement, his free hand sliding to cup her breast. Dibs moaned and panted, Vicki arched and shook, eyes rolling.

"Swan! Swan, she tastes so strong here." Dibs' head popped up long enough for his mate to beam at him, lips shiny, and then Dibs buried his face between Vicki's legs again.

Vicki cried out, hands reaching for him. He slid his hand through her hair, cupping her head as he kissed her. Dibs' hand on his prick tightened, and he remembered to stroke the hard prick that he held. Her sounds pushed into his mouth, louder and louder, almost desperate.

He let go of Dibs' cock, fingers sliding to play with her breasts instead, holding, caressing, playing with the large nipple. Dibs surged up, howling, prick throbbing as he fought to mount her.

"Easy, Dibs," he reminded again. "We have all night." Dibs looked at him like he was crazy. He knew though, that they could drive their Vicki, their mate, into screaming, happy exhaustion.

"Here." He took Dibs in hand again, fingers squeezing as he began to stroke. "We can slow you down this way."

Dibs' eyes crossed and his hips pushed, humping Swan's hand. Vicki's fingers joined his, pumping and stroking Dibs' needy cock. Dibs whined and moaned, hands wrapping around both his and Vickie's shoulders. "Good. Good."

Swan could tell it wouldn't be long, his sweet mate young and quick off the mark. Vicki leaned up, lips on Dibs' throat, teeth threatening. Dibs cried out, bucking hard. Heat spilled over his and Vicki's hands.

"Mmm. Shh. You're good. You're okay." Sweet lover. Swan leaned in, licked her lips, Dibs' throat.

Dibs whimpered softly and then smiled, licking Vick's cheek and then his.

"Better?" Vicki was shifting restlessly, reaching for him.

"Yes. Good." Dibs licked her again.

Leaning back, Swan lowered himself, his prick stiff.

Vicki sat up, pushing up on her elbows, the scent of her hair and her sex flooding him.

"Take me inside you," he told her.

"Demanding man." She moved easily, soft thighs straddling him.

Her skirt billowed out around his hips, and he slid his hands beneath it, fingers wrapping around her waist and guiding her down. Hot and wet, her body wrapped around his cock, drew him in. So different from Dibs' tight heat, and yet she, too, felt wonderful around him. There was no hesitation, nothing but pleasure surrounding him.

He was about to let go of her hips to reach up and take her breasts in his hands, but then Dibs' hands were there, palms cupping, fingers playing.

"I. Oh. Warm." Vicki's head fell forward, moaning softly.

She was beautiful.

She was his, as surely as Dibs was.

Dibs' fingers trailed down, touching where they were joined. He groaned, the sensation of Dibs' fingers on the base of his cock while he was inside Vicki make him buck up.

"She's so wet, slick inside." Dibs groaned softly, touching them both, stroking them.

The touches made him jerk and moan. "She... she is. And hot." So hot.

"Yes," hissed Dibs, one finger pushing in alongside his cock.

Vicki jumped a little, eyes flashing to Dibs. "Oh."

"Hot and wet," Dibs murmured, leaning in to kiss her.

Swan groaned, that finger rubbing against his cock as surely as it was rubbing against Vickie's walls. Her nipples were rubbing against his chest, body fluttering around his cock. Dibs slid open-mouthed kisses over them both, tongue hot as it left wet trails on his body.

"You... you still think you can do this all night, Swan?"

"I may have forgotten just how old I was for a moment," he admitted.

Dibs growled, and swatted his arm. "You can get

it up again."

"For being old, you feel amazing inside me."
Vicki's lips were on his ear, the whisper soft, simple.
Honest.

He smiled at them both, fingers sliding up to
stroke Vickie's cheek, his other hand finding his
sweet Dibs' belly, touching it. He circled his hips
and thrust up.

That whisper became a gasp, Vicki rippling
around him. "Yes."

He thrust again, eyes on hers, watching the pleasure on her face.

"Harder. Harder, Swan. Mate. Please." Mate.

He thrust up harder, Dibs' finger adding sensation.

"Smells so good," murmured Dibs.

She bucked and rolled, heated and fine around
him. Dibs kissed her and then him, and Swan could
taste Vicki in Dibs' mouth. Dibs' hands lifted Vicki's
breasts, fingers working the tight nipples, making
her grip his cock. He called out, Dibs' voice answer-
ing him.

Swan looked to Vicki and called out again. She
responded, looking confused as the sound escaped
her. He and Dibs called back to her, and he could
see the joy on his young mate's face. He lost control
as his pleasure took him, his hips jerking helplessly
as he filled her with his seed. Vicki groaned, taking
him in, holding him tight.

He wrapped one arm around her, the other tugging Dibs in close. "My Pack." They leaned into
him, soft sounds filling the air. "My Pack." It deserved saying again.

Dibs made a soft, happy sound, cuddling right
in. They stroked Vicki's hair, Vicki petting his belly,
Dibs'.

"Are you happy?" he asked Vicki. It was so

many changes for her, all he and Dibs had to do was welcome her in.

"I think I am, Swan. I think I am."

"Good."

Dibs obviously thought so, too, the pup treated both Vicki and him to licks.

He chuckled and let his eyes close.

Happy mates, happy Pack.

Chapter Ten

Dibs was running.

He was running and running and running and maybe if he kept running Vicki wouldn't go because she hadn't said good-bye to him yet.

He wasn't happy.

Not at all.

He didn't understand how Vicki could go.

When he heard Swan barking at him, he ran harder, and then he slowed, letting his Alpha catch up with him. Swan nipped at his heels, turning him, urging him back toward Vicki's house. He didn't want to go. He didn't want Vicki to go.

He yipped and barked and balked until Swan growled and barked once, and then he put on speed and ran as he'd been ordered. He didn't want to, but he ran up onto the back deck, barking at the door.

There was a scent, a wrong scent.

A scared scent.

And something else...

Howling, he called to Swan, to Vicki. Swan's howl answered, followed by barks of warning, Swan beginning to growl.

He could hear sounds inside -- Vicki crying out, crying for them. Swan sailed over him, leaping at the glass door, shattering the brand new window. Dibs followed his alpha in, snarling and barking.

There were three of them, two in wolf form, one as a man, knife at Vicki's throat. "She's ours. We made her."

Dibs growled, hackles rising as Swan shifted, tall and imposing. "You left her. She is my Pack now."

"No. We're taking her." The invader backed away, knife pushing into Vicki's skin.

"She doesn't want to go with you." He could see his Alpha vibrating with the need to jump the knife wielder, to tear out the man's throat.

"Let me go." Vicki was shaking, staring at him, at Swan. Their mate.

THEIRS.

"I will not. You are ours." The big male shook her, her hair falling everywhere.

Dibs leapt, protecting his Pack. Both big males attacked him, teeth and claws tearing, snapping, but it didn't matter. This was his home. His pack. His mate. His. He went for the man's neck, knocking the knife from his hand, teeth snapping on skin. He heard Swan's snarl, knew his mate fought by his side.

One of the wolves went down, kicking and bleeding under his jaws. He heard Vicki's screams turn to snarls and barks. Yes! Fight with us, mate!

The scent of blood was strong, some of it from his Pack, and it made Dibs fight even harder. He tried to get his jaws around the man's neck, but he shifted and Dibs missed, biting into an ear instead. Vicki had the big male's genitals, snapping and biting, blood coming from a blade in her shoulder.

He let go of the ear in his mouth and snapped at the big male's face, taking an eye. He heard a sharp whimper and he turned, pouncing into the fray with Swan and the third wolf.

The big male brushed by them, crashing through the door. The remaining male turned to go, exposing his throat for only a second, but it was enough for Dibs to attack. He closed his teeth around the jugular and held on, the male's own momentum carrying him forward and ripping his throat away.

Blood filled his mouth, the taste of victory hot and salty.

Soft, pained cries filled the air, Vicki scrambling to hide beneath the table, teeth bared. He was beginning to feel aches and pains himself, but he ignored them in favor of going to Vicki, Swan there with him, both of them calling to Vicki, to each other.

Vicki barked, warning them away, so scared. No. No, they didn't want to hurt her. He whined softly. Mates. Couldn't she smell them, smell that they were safe? Swan barked softly, licked his face, cleaning the blood from him. It calmed him and he turned to Swan, whimpering at the wide cut along his Alpha's shoulder.

Swan barked again, and then turned to Vicki, barking to her, the sound an order. Obey your alpha! Vicki snarled, but slunk forward, sliding on the floor. Dibs and Swan both went to her, searching for wounds, licking all over her and trying to get the scent of the others off her. There was a small blade, in her shoulder, the metal smelling wrong with her flesh. Whenever they got close to it, she growled.

Swan shifted, staying low, speaking softly. "It's all right, Vicki. I need to get the blade out."

Dibs barked, worried. Swan was bleeding from a lot of places. Vicki whimpered, head on Swan's thigh as she cried softly, tongue sliding to clean his skin. Dibs snuck in, licking both of them, his own wounds forgotten.

Swan kept murmuring, hand reaching for the knife. Vicki's eyes flashed up to Swan and she keened, so frightened, so sorry that they came for her. "It's okay, Sweet. You didn't know. I'll be quick."

Dibs barked and licked her muzzle. She was theirs. That was all that mattered.

The blade came out and she yelped, jerking away, limping, sliding on the tile.

Swan caught her, sitting hard and holding her in his lap while Dibs licked at the wound, encouraging the skin to knit, to heal. Vicki cuddled in, shaking so hard, sounds pouring from her. Theirs. Their mate.

Dibs put his head back and howled, his pack. Swan and Vicki. Swan's voice joined with his, announcing to the world that this was their territory, their land, their lady.

He settled down next them, one of Swan's hands sliding through his fur. He licked that hand and then focused on the broken glass door. He would make sure no one else came in.

Chapter Eleven

Hurt.

Hurt.

She paced, head tossing and ears twitching at every sound.

Vicki had found a place in a closet, the soft towels and sheets made into a nest in the dark. She hid there, whenever the males left to hunt, to patrol, whenever. She might hide there forever.

Swan came to her, Alpha growling and barking at her, urging her out of her safe nest. He wanted her to come out. Her instincts encouraged her to respond, to obey, and her body moved, even as she growled and barked. Swan led her down to the kitchen, Dibs there with food. He brought her the choicest parts, offering them to her.

Whining softly, she licked his muzzle, Dibs'. So scared. So tired. Both Swan and Dibs licked and barked softly, offering her comfort, love. She curled up between them, eating the food they'd brought, leaning on Dibs, muzzle hidden in Swan's fur.

When the food was gone, they began to lick her, cleaning her wounds yet again. She tried to return the favor, but she couldn't move much and their touches eased her, soothed her.

Loved her.

They nudged her back toward the stairs, helping her up and then pushing her toward the bedroom. Dibs jumped up onto the bed, circling, making a nest for them. She leaned into Swan, vocalizing, telling him how scared she was that the man would come back, how her shoulder hurt, how she couldn't leave now, couldn't leave them.

Couldn't remember how to not be the wolf.

Swan told her she beautiful and safe and theirs. They would protect her. She wasn't going anywhere. And they would help her remember. When it was time. But not today. Today was for sleeping and healing and loving.

He nosed her toward the bed, toward Dibs and the nest of pillows and blankets.
She leapt up, curling into Dibs, nuzzling his belly for a moment. Dibs. Love. Dibs called out, and then licked her, curled with her.

Swan joined them, their alpha keeping them safe, keeping them together.

Vicki sighed, settled, warm, safe.

Home.

Chapter Twelve

Dibs ran through the forest, keeping to a small area around Vicki's house, and the path between her house and their cabin. He went slowly, being careful to scent everything along the way, making sure there were no fresh scents of others.

Swan had fixed the back door. Again. And he and Swan had taken turns guarding Vicki, hunting for food, and patrolling. They were vigilant, not leaving Vicki alone, and making sure no one invaded their territory.

Vicki hadn't changed to human since it had happened. Swan was concerned. Vicki, too. Dibs didn't think that was such a terrible thing, although he did miss some human things. Making love, and showers and lemonade and cake.

Having made his circuit, he loped back to the house, bounding up the stairs and going to the back door, barking to be let in. Swan opened the door as a man, fingers to his lips. Vicki was on the sofa, human, sound asleep.

Dibs shifted as he went in, Swan closing the door behind him. "What happened?"

"She was sleeping and she changed. The wounds are healing well." She was pale, though, face drawn.

"She's going to be okay, isn't she?" He looked to Swan. It might not have been for very long, but she was theirs now and they couldn't lose her. Their pack was three now.

Swan nodded. "She's ours. She's scared, Dibs. So much has changed."

He pressed against Swan. "We'll take care of her."

"We will." Swan's eyes were serious. "Come with me, now. We'll love her."

"It's okay to wake her?" Look at how he was being so good when in fact his prick had jumped up the moment Swan had said they would love her. He waited though, nearly bouncing in place, but he waited for Swan's answer.

"She needs to remember pleasure, Dibs. She needs us."

"Okay!" He could do that. He so very much could.

He kissed Swan first, because, well, because Swan was Swan. And then he bounded to the couch and licked Vicki's face.

Her eyes flashed open, hands reaching for him. "Dibs."

Dibs beamed at her and lay alongside her. His butt stuck out over the edge of the couch, but he was pressed up against her, which felt good.

"Hi, Vicki." He licked her face again.

Her body was warm, soft, so pretty. "It's safe?"

"It is. I checked all around and all the way to our cabin. No new scents. Swan buried the dead one far away. Now we can love you!"

"You're not angry at me?"

"Angry?" Dibs frowned and looked back at Swan to see if he knew what she was talking about. "Why?"

"Because they hurt you. Because of me." Tears started flowing down her face.

"No, don't cry! I'm not mad!" Dibs licked at her tears, washing them from her face.

"It wasn't your fault," Swan added.

"I'm so sorry. I tried to stop them."

"They're gone now." Dibs kept liking and kissing her face, trying to soothe her. He didn't want her to be unhappy!

Swan knelt next to their heads and stroked her hair. "Dibs is right. They're gone now and everybody is going to be fine."

She pressed close against him, head leaning into Swan's touch. "I was so scared that I'd lose you."

"We're Pack. We stick together. We keep each other safe." His licking turned into kisses, pressed over her face.

Her lips opened for him, mouth so sweet, so hungry. He kissed her gently, mindful that she was still healing. At least that was how he started out, but she tasted so good and was so warm that he soon deepened the kiss. She cuddled in, humming a little, body warming up.

Moaning, he pressed even closer, half on top of her, his hands pushing the blankets away so he could touch her. Oh. Oh, he'd missed her. He growled and nuzzled, tongue sliding over her so she smelled like them, like Pack. Swan leaned over them both, hands so good as they touched and rubbed, one on him, one on Vicki.

"Tell me he won't take me."

Dibs growled and pressed closer. "No one will take you. Ours. Our Pack. Our Mate."

"He won't take you." Swan's voice was low, soothing.

"Yours." She reached for them. "My Pack."

Yes.

Yes.

Growling his agreement, he took her mouth again, met Swan's lips, too, as their Alpha bent to kiss them both. The kiss went deep, fiery, the taste of his Pack enough to make him want to howl. Three tongues played together, three sets of lips slid and slipped and pressed against each other.

Dibs began to hump against Vicki's hip. Her skin was smooth, so soft, so fine against his cock. He touched her breasts, still so fascinated by the soft roundness. His thumb brushed over her nipple. That bit of flesh went hard, reaching for his touch, so dark, so lovely. He broke off the kiss, to lean in and take it into his mouth, sucking on the hard flesh.

"Dibs. Dibs, good."

His eyes closed, the rhythmic suction calling something deep and raw inside him. His prick was so hard and he wanted to take her, wanted to be inside her. He slipped one hand down her body, stroking her belly, and then her mound. Her legs spread, dark curls slick and wet against his fingers. He slipped three fingers inside, her body seeming to suck them right in. She cried out into his lips, and then one of Swan's fingers slipped in with his.

Together they brought more and more cries from her, his thumb bumping against the little bundle of nerves each time they pushed in. A dark flush crawled up Vicki's belly, her breath coming faster.

He climbed up between her legs, meeting her eyes. "Love you, Vicki. Mate."

"Mate." Vicki nodded, hands wrapping around his shoulder. "Home."

"Yes." He slid forward, his cock pushing into her.

Her legs wrapped around his hips and he felt Swan behind him, fingers on his ass. Whimpering, he sank deep and then pressed back, eager to have Swan inside him. Forward again, he slid so smoothly within her heat. Vicki moaned for him, called for him. Those sounds made promises to them, things that there weren't even words for.

His slow, easy rhythm stuttered as two of Swan's fingers pushed into him, and then he started up again, riding the sensations in his cock and ass. They found their rhythm, altogether, the three of them moving, dancing, almost running.

Almost without losing a beat, Swan's fingers disappeared and his cock pushed in, spreading Dibs' ass. The burn, the ache -- it was perfect, making him gasp, making him push deep into Vicki.

He whimpered and growled, moving between them. Lucky. He was so lucky to have such a wonderful pack. It couldn't last -- he needed and Vicki was flagging and Swan was growling and nuzzling his nape.

Swan's hand slid between their bellies, rubbing Vicki's bundle of nerves. Dibs could feel her walls tighten around him and he began to howl, his own muscles going tight around Swan's cock as the sound of his pleasure filled the room.

"Love." Vicki cried out, shoulders leaving the sofa cushions.

Swan's howl matched his and he felt the heat from Swan's pleasure push deep inside him. He jerked a few more times, rocking between them, making the good last as long as it could. And then he went still, panting, holding himself up so he didn't collapse onto Vicki.

Vicki's eyes closed, fingers holding him close, holding them together. Swan was a good weight on his back. Dibs lay quietly between them, happy. His pack was altogether, all around him.

It was good.

Epilogue

Swan watched the snow falling down on the forest behind the house. It was the first snows of the season, but it had already been cold for weeks. He had to admit, he liked the advantages of Vicki's house. While it may have been harder to just go run and catch food, Vicki's house had a furnace, different foods, proper insulation and the bed.

Not to mention Vicki was more comfortable there, and she had her work.

He and Dibs were adapting.

They all were.

Vicki was completely healed, as were he and Dibs, their wounds having only been minor, and there had been no sign of the other pack in the intervening months. Swan suspected the wolf who'd turned Vicki had expected to find her alone and unprotected. A coward like that would not return now that he knew there was opposition. Opposition that had managed to kill one of his pack.

Still, he and Dibs patrolled their territory daily, searching for any scents that didn't belong. Dibs had just come in a few moments ago, his patrol having gone very quickly as Vicki had promised something called hot cocoa to go with their cookies when Dibs returned.

He turned at a sound behind him. Dibs was bouncing, eyes wide, white cream on his upper lip. "Swan. Swan. Cocoa is good."

Swan laughed, Dibs' joy infectious as always. "Is it? I hope there's a cup for me." In the meantime, he leaned in and took a taste of the cream from Dibs' lip. Dibs pushed in close, the kiss deepening. His tongue slipped into Dibs' mouth and he could taste a hint of the cocoa there, the taste sweet and just very slightly bitter.

"Vicki smells odd, Swan. She smells different." Dibs whispered into their kiss, eyes warm, happy.

He'd noticed it, too, over the last week or so. "I know. We should ask her about it." He stroked his hand along Dibs' back. Dibs still didn't' like wearing clothes, to him it was fur or nothing. Swan himself preferred the sweatpants and sweatshirt when he was wearing his human skin.

"Is she still in the kitchen?"

"She is. She is making food."

"We are lucky, you know that, Dibs?" She was so good to them, made them such wonderful things to eat.

Dibs bounced and laughed, spilling his hot cocoa over his hand. Still laughing, Dibs licked it away, pink tongue entrancing. "We are! I am -- I have two wonderful mates."

Swan chuckled and headed for the kitchen, Dibs bouncing along with him.

Vicki was standing by the stove, ass shaking side to side as she stirred.

"Sexy!" Dibs bounded right over to her, grabbing her ass with one hand.

"Dibs!" Vicki laughed and pushed into his arms, snuggling into their mate. "Dibs says there's no signs of anyone. Swan? We're safe?"

"We're safe."

"Swan doesn't think he's coming back. Swan says he's a coward." Dibs licked her cheek. "And Swan wants chocolate that's hot."

Swan chuckled. "Dibs is absolutely right. About both the coward and the hot chocolate."

"I just... I worry." She poured him a glass of something hot and steaming.

"We'll keep you safe, Vicki. You're our mate, our pack. But he will not come back." Swan took the glass by the handle and breathed the hot chocolate in. It smelled like Dibs' mouth had tasted, only stronger.

"I hope you're right." Vicki gave Dibs another cup, humming softly.

"I hope so, too." He sipped at his drink, eyes widening. "Oh, this is good!"

Dibs laughed. "I told you!"

"Yes. Yes, you did." He kissed Vicki's cheek. "Thank you." Then he stepped back and looked in her eyes. "Do you have something to tell us?"

"Something?" She had a secret; he could smell it.

"Yes." He pushed the hair off her face, putting it behind her ear. "You can tell us anything, you know, and you will still be ours."

"I just. I'll tell you, Mate. When I'm sure."

Dibs urged her to tell. "Tell us! You smell strange, Vicki."

Swan smiled and nodded at her. "Different. You have a secret."

She nodded to him, and he knew, he could scent it. Babies. There were going to be pups. Oh, he was too old for this.

Still, he couldn't stop the grin that spread across his face. "Our pack is growing."

"It is?" Dibs looked around as if he expected to see someone else walk into the kitchen.

Vicki nodded, stepped closer. "Please tell me he knows where babies come from. That would just be too weird."

"Babies?" Dibs looked at Vicki and then at him. "That's why she smells different?"

Swan nodded, and smiled as Dibs began to bounce, hands going to her tummy. "How many?"

Laughing, Swan took them both into his arms. "You can't smell how many, Dibs."

"Oh." His sweet pup looked most disappointed.

"Only one, I hope. They usually come in ones."

Swan's lips twitched. "But you are part wolf now and we often have more than one baby at a time."

Dibs nodded and bounced, hugging Vicki and then Swan and then Vicki again. "Puppies!"

"Maybe. I'm not sure." Vicki leaned against him, her scent strong, sweet.

Swan slid his hand along her back and Dibs pressed close, fingers stroking her belly. "We are. Trust your instincts, Vicki."

She wouldn't stay in human form long; she'd have a good long run as a wolf, making it easier. Safer. And she had both of them to care for her.

Dibs was obviously over the moon, laughing and kissing and licking her.

Swan tilted her chin to look up at him. "Does it make you happy, Vicki?"

"I... I've never been a mother. I don't know how we'll explain what we are."

Swan laughed. "What we will need to explain to our child will be who those strange humans are and why they cannot shift like we can. We will be what's normal to her. Our Pack."

"The land is paid off. We can stay here, together, all of us." Her breasts were full, nipples hard.

"And at the cabin." It would be easier there, for them to be wolves. They would bring whatever she wanted. And once the baby was born, they could return.

"It's safer there." She reached for them, trembling. "Tell me they won't come back for our babies."

"They won't come back for our babies." He growled out the words. "And if they do I will tear their throats out."

His words relaxed her and she melted between him and Dibs, holding on tight. "Yes. My Pack."

"Pack! Mates! Family!" Dibs bounced and laughed, his joy obvious and wonderful.

"Mine," Swan said softly.

And he would never be too old for that.

For Life
BA Tortuga

Chapter One

"Scootch, Frannie!" Mel tossed the sweet feed
from the truck bed into the barn, her cattle dog barking and bouncing out of the way. Lord, ever since
Len had disappeared in the late spring, Fran'd been
clingy as all get out, just damn near driving her crazy.

Still, Len'd been Fran's littermate and every so
often Mel hoped that sweet boy would show back
up.

She grabbed another bag and tossed, humming
as the wind started blowing, picking up the bottom
of her jack shirt and lifting it enough that the sweat
cooler. It was going to change to the north -- probably bring rain with it too.

Damn good thing she'd put in some good hay.
Come hail or high water, she was going to bunker
down this winter, only go to town for necessities.

No matter what.

Frannie's barking took on a fever pitch, that silly mutt going crazy.

She tilted her head, hopped down from the bed, boots raising a cloud of dust. "What is it, Frannie? Snake?"

Her rifle was sitting on the back seat, waiting for her, and she grabbed it.

Wasn't no snake. Wasn't a coyote, either. It was a big, black and gray wolf, pretty as you please, sitting at the end of the yard. Staring.

She arched an eyebrow, drew back the hammer. "What do you want? This ain't PackLand."

Not even close.

This was her land.

The damned fool just tilted his head, panting a little before sliding down to lie in the dirt, just like some stray dog that had decided to call her place home.

Frannie growled, standing at her leg, all bristled up and all, and Mel caught the stock under her arm, reached down to comfort her. "I ain't in the mood for bullshit. Move on." Strangers weren't welcome here.

The wolf stood again, trotting up toward the house. Her house. Looking back over its shoulder like, are you coming?

"Jesus Christ." She put the tailgate up on the truck and shooed Frannie off toward the barn. The pup would be safe there with the horses. Then she headed to the house, stomping the mud off her boots. Man, she hated getting blood on her front porch.

The wolf went right to her front door, hopping up on the porch and waiting. Ears and tail up.

"Look. I don't know what you want, but I'm NOT friendly, okay? I'm not hunting a mate and I don't need a fuckbuddy or some shiftless cur poaching on my hunting grounds."

A sharp bark was her answer, one big old paw scratching at her door. The message was clear. Let me in.

"Damn it." She twisted her lips, pushed a strand of hair that had come loose from her braid. "I swear by the moon, if you so much as twitch hard, I'll turn your hairy ass into a rug."

Then she opened the door.

As soon as the damned beast got inside he started to change, the furry body lengthening and stretching, going all human and bare. Until she had a big old man sitting on her front rug.

One that looked awfully familiar.

"Hey, Mel," Jamie said. "How's it hanging?"

"Jamie." She just stood there, teeth in her mouth. "Long time no kick your ass."

Naked as a jaybird, he was, and she could understand why he'd wanted in. Not that she wanted to let him, but she could see why. He grinned huge, blue eyes sparkling. "Hey, darlin'."

"Hey. You want coffee?" Pants? A swift kick to the balls?

"I do. We need to chat. You got a towel or something? I kinda had to leave without carrying a bag."

"Yeah. You want some sweatpants? My jeans won't fit your skinny ass."

"That works." He looked her over carefully. "They'd best be your fat pants, though. Your everyday ones won't fit, neither."

"I have a couple pair of guys' sweats, asshole." From the last guy she'd had a fling with. Fucker.

"Yeah?" One black brow rose to Jamie's hairline. "Do tell."

She felt her cheeks heat and, fuck, didn't that piss her off. "It ain't none of anybody's. I don't answer to folks these days."

She headed to the laundry room and grabbed a

towel and a pair of pants. She tossed them to Jamie and then stomped to the kitchen, fixing a pot of coffee.

Jamie.

Shit.

She hadn't seen him in what? Ten years? Maybe more. He looked good. Hard-bodied, scarred, tanned. Good.

Hell, she hadn't seen him or Rick, Billy, Kelly, Brett -- none of them. That was what happened when kids grew up and got bitchy. Everything went away.

"You look good, Mel"

He stood in the doorway, leaning, sweats hanging low.

She snorted. She looked like her, plain and simple. "What you been up to, man?"

"This and that. Lately? Been on the road. So to speak." He had chest hair. Man, when had that happened?

"How do you take your coffee?" Her eyes kept going to that little line of muscle, pointing down into the sweats...

"Black, darlin'. How about you? What are you up to?" Jamie wandered into the kitchen, touching this and that.

"Working the horses. Working the cattle." Staying under the radar. She poured the coffee, adding a little creamer to hers. "Why are you here, Jamie?"

"Well..." He rubbed his thumb over his chin. "We got a problem."

She felt her eyebrows raise up. The last time she'd heard that she was young and wild and dying for a good time.

"In fact, have you heard from anyone lately?" Something serious darkened those eyes, made his brows lower.

"Anyone like who? I haven't seen one of our kind in years. Maybe since we all went our separate ways."

"Damn." Jamie shook his head, taking the cup of coffee she offered. "We may be the last two."

"The last two what?"

"Of the old pack, honey. Everyone I've tried to contact but you is dead." He said it so casually that to begin with, she didn't understand.

"What? That cain't be right." No way. There'd been damn near twenty of them. Twenty. "It is some cancer or something?"

"No." Sighing, Jamie sipped his coffee, humming his appreciation. "No, that would be easier."

"Okay, quit beating around the fucking bush and just tell." She wasn't good at playing games and there was a sick feeling in the pit of her stomach.

"Some kind of hunters, honey. I've tracked down everyone but Brett, now. You're the only one alive." Jamie grimaced, swallowing more coffee, Adam's apple bobbing like he was queasy. "It wasn't pretty."

"Hunters?" She frowned, went to the front door and whistled for Frannie, who came right in. Then she locked the door. "What kind of hunters? What're they looking for?" What the fuck?

"Well, I haven't had much time to figure on it. I've been traveling fast and light, every since I got a message from Billy's people."

She could see Billy -- all red-headed and goofy, laughing at her and Brett and Jamie doing some goofy truck surfing stunt.

"You sayin' little Billy's..." No. No fucking way.

His faced screwed up, his shoulders hunching. "Yeah. Yeah, Mel. He had a wife..."

She stepped back, gorge rising, fingers balling

into fists. "Who the fuck's hunting us?" She had herself one hell of an aim and she wasn't a stranger to hunting.

"Honey, I have no idea. And if it was just Billy, I'd think it was a coincidence." Tossing the rest of the coffee into the sink, Jamie rolled his head on his neck. "I have to find Brett if I can, but the moon's too close."

She nodded, chewing on her bottom lip. "You know where he is?" They had two nights, including tonight, but that was it.

"I think. It'll take too long to get there." Sometimes Jamie and Brett had tied it up, but she could tell Jamie didn't want their old buddy to come to harm.

"Okay." Did Jamie just come to warn her? Did he need somewhere to stay? "You hungry?"

She needed to make some plans.

"I am. I'm starving." Jamie came and put his hands on her shoulders, and they were bigger than she remembered. Stronger. "I'm glad you're okay, honey."

It was easy to wrap her arms around his waist, hug him tight. "Damn, Jamie. Just... Damn."

"I know, honey. I know. I..." He kissed her cheek and popped her butt, stepping back. "Feed me, woman."

Yeah. Jamie wasn't ever one for emotional scenes.

"Don't make me kick your ass, man." She headed to the kitchen and pulled out the steak she'd defrosted. There was enough meat for two, if she did rice and gravy. She grabbed herself a beer and washed her hands. She needed to get to the feed store and stock up on ammo.

"Got another one of those? I think I might have hit my coffee limit." Well, that was new. Jamie had been able to drink the shit by the vat, once upon a time.

"Sure." She handed one over and started cooking, her shoulders so tight they screamed.

Jamie stood back and watched, sipping his beer, staring out the window every so often like he was watching his backtrail. Fucking unnerving.

"Are they on your tail, Jay?" Did they follow you here? And who the fuck were they?

"I don't think so, honey. Not yet. I was deep in the Rockies, and I took nothing with me. Hopefully, they're still looking for me." He shrugged, face carefully blank.

"Well, I'll be ready for them, should they come." This was her land, goddamn it.

"You think? Billy was in a pack of ten, honey." His voice became a low growl. "Ten."

Her knife came down, slicing her finger. "Fuck."

Ten.

"Shit, babe." He was right there in a split second, grabbing a towel and putting it over the cut. He obviously couldn't stop himself from scenting the blood, though.

"Sorry." Her nostrils flared a little and then, all of the sudden, the wolf was there, dragged to the surface by the nearly full moon, the steak, the blood, and Jay. Right there.

Jamie shook a little, hands clamping down on hers, the skin wavering a little. She groaned, growled low, her lips parted as she fought to keep her shit together.

Jamie finally just brought her finger up and licked it, tongue scraping across her skin. Oh, that was so not helping.

Her muscles rippled, the world going from bright colors to pure scent and sensation. She could smell male wolf, could feel the air ripple as Jay came with her. Everything became fur and the wild urge to run.

She headbutted him, muzzle sliding against his. Pack. Pack. She'd missed him!

Licking her nose, Jay whined, low in his throat, body bumping against hers. His eyes glowed for her, his teeth closing on her ear gently.

She hopped up on the counter, tugging the meat down onto the floor, barking happily. Eating, then running.

Jay came after her, chasing her tail, his big paws sounding like thunder against her floor. Frannie barked at them from the front room, staying far away. He'd grown. She ducked under his forelegs, scrambling away to steal a chunk of meat, snapping it up happily. Growling, Jay snapped back, trying to take her down, but it was all play. She knew that sound.

He might be bigger, but she was faster, and she zoomed around him, claw skittering on the tile.

They smacked up against the cabinets, slamming against the trashcan, which stopped Jay for just long enough for her to skitter out the doggie door.

She took off like a shot, scrambling across the pasture, muscles burning.

Jay ran right behind her, then beside her, nipping at her ear again. Probably to let her know he was the big male. She threw herself against him, hoping surprise would knock him over if her weight didn't.

Skidding, Jay barked, tongue lolling in a toothy smile before he caught his balance and headed right back for her.

Damn it. She took off, claws digging into the dirt, chuffing happily as they played.

They were playing king of the hill behind the barn when a brown blur shot past her, knocking Jay off the little knoll he stood on, barking. A sharp yelp sounded, Jay rolling over and over in the dirt.

Her ruff puffed up and she snarled, scrambling to her feet. Her land. Her territory.

HERS.

The big brown male stood over Jay, barking and snarling, snapping his teeth. He never even looked at her. She leapt without thinking, teeth grabbing the brown male's ruff as she flew by.

He took her right down, slamming her to the ground. Then he closed his teeth on her throat, so gently that she hardly felt it. Like he was family.

She chirruped, sniffing. Eyes going wide.

Brett.

Their Brett.

She scrambled to her feet, staring, panting at the males.

What the hell?

Jay sniffed around them, limping the tiniest bit, but not at all growly about it. He knew, too. Knew it was Brett.

Mel stared, vibrating in place. Then she headed over to Brett, licking his chin. Barking, Brett licked her nose before whirling to snap at Jay again. Jay backed off, tail up and head down, daring Brett to come and get him.

She watched, slowly heading toward her house, never looking away from them. They bounded after her, running ahead, racing. Just like always. She switched between playing back and growling, confused, her simple routine just torn to hell.

The boys finally wore out and went to lie down on the porch, both panting like fools. Idiots.

She pushed inside, shaking off the wolf with difficulty, ending on her knees in the kitchen. Frannie'd eaten the steak and the rice was burned. Figured.

Mel grabbed herself a beer and headed for the

master bath, locking the door and turning the water on as hot as she could stand it.

Maybe if she closed her eyes, she could pretend the fucking world wasn't turned upside down.

***

Brett woke up on Mel's porch, naked and sunburned. Goddamn. Jay was nowhere to be seen, even though they'd fallen asleep together. Asshole, going in and leaving him out there.

His wolf was gone, his body too exhausted to call it up so he could get into the doggie door. He tried the handle, finding the damned door locked, the dog barking up a storm.

Shit. He'd just have to knock.

Nobody showed up, but he heard footsteps, a soft low whistling. "Come on, Frannie. I got to get to town and buy food for the next couple days. Outta my way. The boys ain't going to bite you. Just don't let 'em near your hind end."

"You could let me in." Damn it, he'd bet she was enjoying this.

"I could." She appeared behind him, stomping up the back porch steps. "Jay lock your happy ass out, man?"

She reached up, fingers sliding over the back door, coming up with a key. "Here we go."

"Oh, hey." Well, at least she hadn't been the one to leave him hanging in the wind. "How goes, Mel?"

"Busy. You?" She looked good -- she'd gotten curvier, blonde hair long and pulled back, ass covered in tight denim.

God, she looked good. Smelled good, too. "Well, I was doing just fine until about two weeks ago."

"Yeah? What happened?" She poured him a cup

of coffee, poured herself one. There was one still on the counter.

"Someone killed Billy, Mel. Him and his whole pack." He met her eyes, trying to ease the blow.

"Jamie said. Jamie said all of us were dead." Her lips went tight, brow furrowing. "I'm going to town today; buy ammo and food and stuff."

"You should let one of us go with you." Where the hell was Jamie anyway? Damned asshole. Couldn't even say hello as a human.

"There's no decent clothes here. I'll have to get some at the Wal-Mart. You want an egg or something?"

"Yeah. That'd be good." His belly rumbled, reminding him how many miles it had been since he'd eaten. "Thanks."

She nodded, digging out eggs and sausage and an old pan, working like she was a million miles away.

"Hey." Brett reached out, put a hand on one round hip. "You could say hi. Proper like."

"I." She turned, looking at him, searching his eyes. Lord, she looked tuckered. "Hi." Then Mel just stepped close, arms wrapping around him and hugging him tight.

Breathing in her scent, he hugged her back hard. "Hey, Melon. Missed you."

"Yeah." She chuckled a little. "Nobody's called me Melon in ten years, you big ass."

"No? Well, then you needed it." His fingers wandered down to pinch her butt. He couldn't help it.

"Fuckhead." Her laughter rang out and she swatted him hard on his bare ass, her hand stinging. "Let me make y'all some food so I can get to town."

"I can make eggs if you have something..." He'd almost forgotten he was naked. "An apron?"

"I have some old shorts. They're not great, but

they'll protect your willie." She patted it, casual as anything, then headed to a little laundry room and started pulling down boxes of old clothes.

Laughing, Brett grabbed the eggs and started cracking, doing enough for Jay, too, who was bound to show up when stuff started sizzling.

"So, what is this? The naked chef?" Speak of the devil.

"I'm hunting clothes. Did you figure out the shower?" A pair of shorts got tossed to him. "Sausage or bacon?"

"Bacon," he and Jay said in unison, grinning at each other.

"Assholes." Well, hell. Bacon got her bent over, ass wiggling as she dug in the fridge.

Brett watched appreciatively, his hands stilling where they were beating eggs. Damn. She looked fine.

Jamie stepped up next to him, staring. Looking a little stunned.

"Uh-huh." They shared another look, both of them shaking their heads. Then Jamie looked down at him.

"Put on your shorts, man. You're gonna burn that, sticking out that way."

Oh, damn. Mel stood up, two packages of bacon in hand. "What are y'all going on about?"

"Nothin'." He turned ever so casually and pulled the shorts on, figuring giving them a show of his ass was better than the pokey.

Jamie was chuckling and Mel nudged them out of the way, the bacon slapping into the pan.

Since he couldn't grab Mel and carry her off to his cave, Brett settled for slugging Jay in the stomach, which led to Jamie whacking him across the chin. They crashed into the little breakfast table maybe five seconds later, both of them swinging.

The spray of icy cold water made him gasp, Mel standing there with the spray hose from the sink, soaking them.

They rolled in opposite directions, both of them coming up on hands and knees, blinking.

"What the hell did you do that for, Melon?"

"Yeah." Jamie shook water out of his hair. "I had him."

"This is my fucking house. No fighting. No breaking shit. No being assholes!" She was getting loud. "You both come here and tell me that everybody else is gone and..." She stopped, dropped the hose like it was a snake. "I'm going to town. I'll buy y'all some jeans. Don't burn the bacon."

Then Mel just headed for the door.

It clicked shut behind her, and Brett sighed, scrubbing a hand through his hair. "She's got a point. Did you... She said you knew."

"Yeah. I was... They're hunting us. You two are the ones I couldn't find."

"Well, you found Melon." So had he. Which meant all manner of other folks could, too. "She planning on digging in?"

"Yeah. She... she's living like a hermit, huh? Our wild girl?" Jamie gave him a confused grin. "She says she won't leave. I was coming to find you, when the moon waned."

"Well, now I'm here." Brett clapped Jay on the shoulder. "I'm proud that you were coming for me, though. I really am."

"Like I wouldn't, man." Jamie sniffed. "Save the bacon."

"Shit." Bacon, eggs, Jamie made toast, and they even found some milk. He fucking loved milk. Of course, he liked cow better.

They sat at the little table with its stack of napkins and stack of mail and little stack of dog-eared novels. The house was... strangely Melody and not, all at once. She'd liked being outside, even then, and the whole place was done up in purples and blues. But the wild-child? The fun? That edge of pure evil? He couldn't see that here.

Maybe she had just been determined to stamp it all out of her. Hell, he could relate, even if he'd never lost the urge to start trouble. He had twinges of conscience now and again. Pesky shit, that conscience.

"So..." Jamie stared at him. "You just gonna leave her here to face 'em?" That was Jay -- he never did beat around the bush worth a shit.

"Hell, no. We're together, huh?" That had to mean something. "We always were better as a set."

He got a wicked grin, Jamie's foot bumping his under the table. "Good. I wouldn't want to have to choose between you."

Laughing, he nudged back, loving the gleam in those blue eyes. "You never could."

"Nope. She's still a fierce, fine bitch." Those eyes slid over his chest, shining, hunger in the air.

"She is. Did you see her ass?" The scent of musk caught him, his nose lifting automatically.

"Fuck, yes. Saw yours, too, had a pretty little girly handprint on it."

"She got me good." He'd deserved it. Brett moved a little closer, hand falling on Jay's leg. "I didn't get to see yours."

"Nope." Jay's nostrils flared and he could hear the low, deep rumble calling for him.

Brett rumbled right back, his hand sliding up Jamie's leg, right up to where those soft sweats hid nothing. Not a damned thing. Jamie spread like butter for a hot knife, wanting him, just like always.

"Damn. Been a long time, man." He slid right off the chair, landing on his knees to yank Jay's pants down, letting that pretty cock out.

"It has." Jay's hands stroked over his face, calluses rough and heavy.

"Working hands." He grinned, breathing the man in for all he was worth before letting his mouth close over the tip of Jamie's cock.

The sound that pushed out of Jamie's mouth went right to his cock, heavy and deep and just happy as all get out. Hell, he was pretty happy. It had been a long time for him, in any way, doing the whole lone wolf thing like he had been. Closing his eyes, Brett sucked hard, all the way down.

Those hands pushed through his hair, then moved to touch his face, his throat. Lord, Jamie was always on the damn move, always shifting and sliding and pushing up toward him. Brett just took whatever Jay was willing to give, lips sealing tight. God, it had just been so damned long. So damned lonely.

"Good. Oh, man. Fucking hot." Yeah. Yeah, they were, Jamie's prick spreading his lips.

Humming his approval, Brett went to town, his hands sliding all over that fine body.

It wasn't going to be long, not at all. He could taste Jay, sliding down his throat, burning his tongue. Growling, he encouraged Jamie to come for him, to give him what he needed. He could still smell Mel's scent, and it only added to the pleasure.

Bitterhotsaltymale. Jay poured into his lips, the happy howl ringing out in the dining room. Brett closed his eyes and let it take him, let himself swallow Jay down, even as his hips rocked up. His cock was harder than it had been in years, and it only took one touch of his hand to bring him off.

Jay's hand curled around his nape, tugging him up into a fierce, sharp kiss. Uhn. Brett all but crawled up into the man's lap, pushing right into that kiss, growling into it. Taking it over. Control passed back and forth, the growling and fury growing, getting sharper.

They toppled out of the chair, rolling across the floor, biting at each others' lips. He landed on top, just like he always had, snarling, teeth on Jay's throat. His. Jay bared everything for him, head tipping back, belly arching up. Yes. His. All over the place.

He swiped his hand up along Jay's body, claws barely scoring the tanned skin.

"Brett!" Jay was just bucking beneath him, rubbing, their scents mingling.

They kissed hard enough that blood spilled, their tongues lapping it up.

Goddamn. He could do this forever. He so could. Well, except that then his dick would fall off. And that would be a shame, 'cause Mel wasn't home yet.

"Oh, man." The thought of Mel and Jay had him humping again, biting, growling a little. Fuck, yes.

"Mmm. Fucking hot. You think we could move to the sofa before we fuck, man? I'll get carpet burn on my butt bone."

"Hell, yes." They were gonna fuck. His whole body kinda went sproing, and Brett took off like a shot, racing for the couch.

Jay scrambled behind him, feet slapping on the floor, tackling his ass by the sofa. They rolled and hit up against the couch with a thud, the lower part of an arm digging into his back. Brett pushed off it, rolling Jay over, straddling him again. Jay barked for him, baring those white teeth, challenging him.

Oh, he was so gonna have that ass. He bent, nuzzling, then biting at that long throat, wanting to just howl his pleasure. Jamie tasted so fucking good -- like pack and home and everything fucking right with the world. Those hands knew him, too, knew where to touch, where to pet him so that he damn near screamed with it.

His back arched, his cock full and hard, and he only paused long enough to haul Jamie's ass up on the couch. Those muscled legs wrapped around him, dragged him closer. Damn, somebody was hot as a firecracker. Their bodies slapped together again, both of them tussling for control. Goddamn. His hips started rocking, his fingers clutching at those lean hips.

He got Jay tilted, got that ass right where he needed it, cock head nudging that tight hole.

Brett's eyes tried to roll. "Ready, man? I can't wait. I don't have anything..."

"I didn't break the first time, Brett."

"No." No. God knew, if Jay hadn't died that first time, he never would. That had been rough and stupid and so hot he still jerked off to it.

"Fuck me. Missed it. Missed y'all."

"Yeah. God, yeah." One stupid mistake and you went years without this kind of heat. Brett pushed inside, slamming home, his head falling back on a howl.

Jay's claws scraped down his shoulders, teeth bruising against his throat as that amazing tight little body held on tight. Brett thrust harder, moving them along the couch, both of them scrambling a little for purchase.

He could feel Jay's little cries and growls against his skin and, fuck him raw, those hadn't changed in years. Jay still had that pure physical joy, that same love of life. That same absolute need. Brett took all of it he could. As much as he fucking took, Jamie just gave, laughing and howling.

God, yeah. They rocked and moved and bit, and made sure their claws didn't dig into the couch. Mel would kill them.

They settled into a good, hard rhythm, his cock pushing and pulling and slamming into that sweet fucking ass.

Jay went crazy for him, pushing back, taking him all the way in, and Brett moaned, just giving it all he had. "Come on, Jay. Come on."

"Yeah. Yes. Fuck, it's good." Heat sprayed between them, wet and fine, Jay's ass like a vise.

"Christ!" He came as hard as he ever had, like a ton of bricks, like he hadn't a few minutes ago. Jesus.

Jay's arms landed on the small of his back, holding tight.

"Mmm." They'd have to figure out what to do, soon. Have to make a plan in case they couldn't make a stand. This, though? This would do for right now.

It was pretty damned good.

Chapter Two

Her house smelled like a fucking whore house. Jesus Christ. She couldn't leave them two alone for four hours...

Still, she was loaded for bear. Ammo. Food. Water. Ammo. Clothes for the boys. Medical supplies. Feed for the animals. Wire to run an invisible fence.

She dumped off her first load, throwing a window open on her way back out. Fucking slut boys.

"Hey, lady." Jay came out, hair all mussed, blinking, his sweats a little torn. Damn.

"Hey, Jay. Y'all get some rest?" She grabbed a fifty-pound bag of dog food, hauled it over her shoulder and headed for the woodbox. It was as good a place as any for it.

"Some, yeah." Grinning, Jay came on out to help her, hauling shit to the porch.

Man, it was hard to be pissed. Hell, it was Jay. She never had been able to stay aggravated with that son of a bitch. So, Mel didn't bother. "I got you some clothes, Jay. And some donuts."

Brett, now. Brett popped out with his bright eyes and even brighter smile, and that was enough to piss her off. "Oh. Donuts."

"Did I say that the donuts were for you, old man?" She grabbed another set of bags, headed for the house.

"Shee-it. When am I the old one?" Brett waited until she let down her load before grabbing her and hugging her tight, nose buried in her hair.

Oh.

She damn near cried, more from the way she felt shocked and odd about being touched after so long, than from the fact that Brett was hugging her. She didn't bother doing it, though. No, she just grabbed a hold of the feeling and let it happen.

"You're feeling good these days, Melon," he said quietly, almost patting her butt. Not quite.

"Hard work and simple living's good for a body." Jesus, she sounded like Granny.

"Uh-huh." He grinned against her neck. "I wonder what Jay's excuse is."

"He's a sweet goofball and the universe is good to those." She peeped as Jay popped her ass. "Hey!"

"No badmouthing me. I would like to note that I got here first." Jay grinned. "Think you got enough ammo?"

"I sure as shit hope so. Got feed and supplies, too, in case I have to hole up for a bit, stay low."

"We're gonna stay and help," Brett said, hugging her again before spinning away to pace to the end of the porch.

"You..." She stood there, mouth open. "What?"

"Did I stutter?"

Jay sighed and put an arm around her waist. "Y'all stop. We're gonna hang out, honey. Might as well, huh?"

"Don't you fucking snap at me, asshole. This is my place. I'll not turn you away, because you're Pack and God knows I love y'all to death, but don't start fucking playing Alpha here. I won't have it."

Jay's eyes went wide, and the man backed up a step, hands up, but Brett knew who she was talking to. He grinned over his shoulder. "You won't have it, huh? Well, I can't promise, but I'll try to keep the balls tucked, babe."

"Well, you know, if you ask Jay real nice, maybe he'll stretch them a little and shove them up your ass for you." She fought her own grin, but lost. "Sweetheart."

Throwing his head back, Brett laughed right out loud, the sound deep and rich. "How defensible are you?"

"Depends on how they come in." It only took a step before she could lean against the banister -- and Jay -- a little. "If they come up the road, there's one way in and they have to cross the bridge. If they come through the pastures... It'll be harder."

"Okay, so we know they won't come over the bridge."

Jay nodded, leaning back, his hand on her hip. He was such a snuggle-bunny. Always had been.

"My closest neighbor is three hundred acres away to the south." There was a sick, sour feeling in the pit of her stomach. "It's commercial farms north and east. Cattle to the south. North is the road."

"We can work with that, Melon." Brett was right there all of a sudden, hugging up on her and Jay, his scent soothing as anything.

"Who's hunting us, baby? I mean, we fucking lost everything in the..." She shook her head; she didn't think about back then. About that life. There was nothing be madness for her back there.

Madness and blame.

"I don't know. I've got the word out, looking. People who don't know you, don't know where we are." Brett squeezed and Jay crowded in, and before she knew it they were on the porch on their knees, sort of a puppy pile of mammoth proportions.

Mel couldn't quite catch her breath, her boys. They smelled so good and she'd missed them, like a lost limb. Brett murmured something like that right into her ear, his lips hot and soft. Jamie was always so much more eager, and he pressed against her, growling a little.

"Y'all." She leaned into Jamie's body, turned her head to meet Brett's eyes.

"We'll figure it, Melon. I promise. I won't leave you hanging." No. No, he never had, even when things went to hell. That had been the problem.

"Well, then." She reached out, touched his lips. "I reckon you can have donuts, too."

"Oh, good. You know how much I like a donut." He kissed her fingers, tongue flicking out to taste her a little.

"I do." She couldn't have stopped her moan if she'd tried, electricity shooting up her arm and spreading through her.

"Hey, still here," Jay said, muscling in a little, kissing her right on the mouth.

Oh, Jay. She knew that taste, right down to her bones, Jamie's hands sliding around her waist. Brett was right there, too, pushing into the kiss, tongue pressing right in between. Asserting himself a little.

Fuck, they made her head swim. She got one hand on Jamie's shoulder, the other landing on Brett's thick, solid thigh.

"Mmm." Jamie's moan vibrated right through the kiss, his cock pushing against her hip, hot even through the cloth. Brett laughed, pushing a hand down between them to touch.

Mel nipped at Brett's bottom lip, caught herself turning to get her hands in on all that strong, male flesh. "Y'all are a damn temptation."

She really ought to unpack all her bags of stuff, damn it.

She could wait just a little longer, though. Especially when Jamie scooted around behind her, supporting her against his chest while Brett's lips slid down her neck. Her toes curled, ass arching back toward Jamie, breasts pushing against Brett. The assholes knew all her hot spots, knew how to derail her.

Brett chuckled, kissing her lips, his tongue pressing in again. Jay just laughed against her neck, licking and sucking, his hands sliding around to cup her through her shirt. She shuddered a little and her lips opened, and damn if Brett didn't press in, kiss her so hard the world did a curtsey to the left.

His mouth was hot, salty, tasted like Jay. Oh, Lord. Jamie was damned busy, too, rubbing against her butt, moaning all along her skin. Somebody's fingers were working her jack shirt open, somebody else's were opening her jeans, tugging at her belt.

"So pretty," Brett said, licking her lower lip. "So damned hot, Mel. I missed you. Missed this."

"God yes. Like a lost tooth. My boys." She shivered as her tank top was pushed up.

"Yours," Jay agreed, while Brett growled and nipped at her. Then two sets of hands were easing off her bra, both of her boys rubbing at her, thumbs on her nipples.

Her hands didn't know where to light. They both felt good and she needed to touch them both. Kiss the curve of Jay's belly. Bite Brett's shoulder.

"Mel..." Jamie rubbed along her hip, turning with her again, his bristly chin digging into her shoulder. His hands slid up and down, dragging along her skin even as Brett pulled her closer.

"Yeah. Y'all are a fucking embarrassment of riches." They all laughed at the joke, and then they all pushed together for a kiss, tongues and lips greedy, hungry.

Brett reached around her to touch Jay, his big, square hand looking brown as anything against her skin and Jay's. The man hadn't lost an ounce of his intensity. Not one.

Mel just didn't know where to look. What the fuck to do that wouldn't make her just pop with it. Brett got her jeans off, his mouth on her belly, his lips hot as fire. Jay was right there, loving on her, his mouth on her breast.

The porch was cool under her, but she wouldn't

have cared if it were freezing, she was caught right there, those mouths making her world tilt. "More. Please, y'all."

"What do you want, honey?" Jay asked. He always asked. Brett just knew, pushing between her legs and opening her right up, his tongue finding her most sensitive spot.

"Oh!" She arched, heat flooding her in a rush. Jamie covered her lips with his, stealing her breath while Brett turned her into a flaming pile of need.

They moved like they were on some weird mental wavelength, like they had a plan in advance. She knew better, though. Neither one of them was a long-term thinker. They didn't have to be. That was her fucking job.

Of course, she didn't have to worry about... "Oh. Oh, fuck. I... Just like that."

Licking at her, Brett pushed closer, breathing her in, all but eating her right up. Then Jamie's mouth got hold of her nipple again, pulling good and hard, and she screamed with it, just hollered with it.

They drove her higher and higher, sent her flying, Brett's tongue pushing inside her, pressing deep. Everything went fuzzy and shit, pleasure crashing over her, again and again, then someone pushed long, hard fingers inside her, and it drove her higher.

"Come on, Mel." Jay's breath felt steamy hot on her lips as he urged her on. Brett wasn't talking. His mouth was damned busy.

"Uh. Uh-huh. Y'all..." She shook as she melted, moaning and shuddering, coming so hard she felt a little broke.

"That's it, baby. That's it." Brett said it against her thigh, panting for her, hot and sweet. Jay was moving, grunting, working toward his own pleasure.

"C'mere." She tugged Brett up, his cock bumping against her, begging in, and she let it, let him, even as Jay swooped over to take Brett's mouth in a kiss.

Brett moaned, his hips punching up, cock sliding right into her. His hands found Jay's shoulders, clinging, and he damned well fucked them both, her with his cock, Jay with his tongue.

She shifted, turned her head, getting Jamie's cock in her hand, closer to her lips.

"Oh, God." Jay thrust at her, his groan loud against Brett's cheek. Brett nodded, chuckling, moving faster. Daring them both to stop.

Jamie tasted just like she remembered, wild and sweeter than Brett. She used to tell them Jamie tasted less growly. She got her lips around the crown of Jay's cock, sucking and tugging, trying to match Brett's thrusts.

Brett was thicker, hotter. Jay was longer. Some things just felt like yesterday, like they'd never been away.

Some things, though? Some things were new. Like the way Jamie moved, slow and sure, like he wanted to feel her mouth forever. Or the way Brett's hand cupped her hip, kept her from rubbing on the porch. They were way more careful of her now, and it was somehow way sweeter. Hotter. Less frenzied and more a deep burn. Brett spread her almost impossibly, pulled her up on his thighs.

Fuck, she had missed this. Missed them. Needed. She moaned around Jamie's cock, toes curling. Jay gave her more, pushing between her lips, rocking her against Brett. Brett was greedy, sliding in and out of her, making her so wet, so hot, she thought she might just explode.

Then Jay's hand slipped down her belly, heading right for her clit and rubbing. Then she did go nuts, bucking and sucking and going to town.

Brett shouted for her, coming hard inside her, his cock impossibly hard and wide. Jay almost slipped out of her mouth as he bucked against her, but Brett caught him, holding Jamie right there.

Come on. Come on, Jay. You too. All of us. She swallowed hard, demanding all her men could give her.

Jay cried out, spilling into her mouth, his balls drawing right up against his body. Oh, yeah. That was it.

They all slumped on the porch, panting, groaning. She had Jay's salt on her lips. Brett kissed her hard, searching out Jay's flavor, and that might have been hotter than anything else they'd done.

Damn. Damn, she still loved the miserable, beautiful sons of bitches.

"Maybe we should unload the rest of the stuff, huh?" Jamie kissed her cheek, laughing like a loon.

"I reckon. Y'all prob'ly want some clothes on and all."

"Oh, clothes can be overrated," Brett rumbled, but he got up, helping her up, helping her right her clothes.

"Yeah, but the way beef is priced now, them steaks aren't." She swayed a little, sore in places she hadn't been sore in for a long, long time.

"Beef..." Jay had that hallelujah look on his face. "Come on, then!"

She chuckled. "Beef, chicken, coffee, donuts -- enough to keep us a bit."

All of them.

Here. Safe. Waiting to see if the hunters found them.

***

Jamie woke up feeling bruised and battered, but

in the best way he could imagine. He stretched hard, yawning, his muscles singing with delicious pain.

Damn. He had missed Mel and Brett, for sure. Both of them, in different ways.

He couldn't miss them now, though, not piled together in Melon's bed like they were. Tangled. Fucking A.

Melody's lips were swollen, red like she'd put lipstick on. There was a hickey on one breast, right by her nipple, another on her hip. Brett's fingers were curled around his thigh, tangled in Mel's hair, and he followed that long arm up, counting the bite marks, the bruise. He could feel matching bruises throbbing on his own skin.

"Mmm." Brett shifted, rubbing along Mel's side, hand squeezing his leg. "Morning."

"Hey." He grinned down, winked as Mel stretched under that touch. "She's still fucking fierce."

"You know it. Still our Melon, huh?" He got a nice good morning, Brett leaning over Mel to give him a kiss.

Mel turned over, stretching hard, rocking underneath them a second. "Gotta feed."

"Feed what?" they asked in perfect harmony, Mel's snort ringing loud. "We'll help," Jamie went on, kissing her shoulder.

"Mmm." She stretched again, head down, butt up, toes curled tight.

Lord, look at that sweet, round ass. He did love how she'd filled out. Damn. Jay copped a feel, completely unable to help himself. His hand ran right into Brett's and they both looked at each other, chuffing a little.

"Y'all laughing at me?"

"Nope. We're just single minded," Brett said, thumb rubbing over his fingers.

"You mean you have one to share between

you?"

He swatted her good, hand leaving a pretty pink mark on her butt. Brett growled at him a little, nipping at him over Mel's shoulder. Possessive bastard.

Mel leaned and bit his leg, hard enough that it stung. "No spanking."

"Not even a little? Just a tiny smack?"

"Sure. A tiny one." Brett's hand landed on his ass, hard, making him yelp.

Mel's laughter stung a little, too, but she soothed that by sliding up along his side, nuzzling his chest. "Morning."

"Hey, you." Jamie wrapped around Mel a little, pulling her up for a kiss, too.

He loved her little sounds, how she cuddled in and hugged him good morning.

God, it was good to be back with them. It was always Brett and Mel for him. The rest had just been window dressing. It'd damn near killed him to walk away from them and he knew they felt the same, running in the middle of the night.

"Someone is thinking too much," Brett said, sliding a hand over his hip. "We're basking. 'Kay?"

Mel nodded, lips sliding over his throat, his jaw. "This is ours, Jay-love. Ours."

Jamie settled a little, licking at Mel's mouth, Brett's cheek. "Okay, okay. I'll stop thinking so loud."

"Good." Mel chuckled, fingers sliding down his stomach. "There's way more fun to get into."

"Yeah?" He could go for a lot of fun. Jamie stretched out a little, let Mel and Brett have at him.

Mel stretched out along one side, cheek on his shoulder, fingers tugging his short hairs.

"Uhn." Shit, that got a rise out of him right away, and when Brett moved down to lick at his belly, he groaned, humping a little. Damn.

"Mmm. So fine." Mel had gone all sex and need, eyes heavy-lidded, lips full and swollen as she touched him.

"Melon..." God, he loved her eyes, her mouth. He cupped one breast in his hand, lifting it gently, thumb rubbing across the nipple.

It went tight for him, and her hips rolled, sliding against him and bumping Brett. Hell, yes. Brett laughed, the warm, damp air of it blowing over his skin. The man was still oral as hell, licking at them, sucking his belly, then Mel's hipbone.

"Never does have enough to fill his mouth, does he?" Mel was a wicked, wicked bitch, gasping as Brett nipped at her.

"Nope. He's always hungry."

"I'll show you two hungry," Brett growled, swarming over them, biting and licking at their skin.

Mel met Brett halfway, laughing and poking, tickling them both.

"Stop! Shit, stop!" Jay flailed, his ribs starting to hurt, he was laughing so hard.

She blew a raspberry on his belly, and then Brett's lips caught Mel's, the kiss hard and hungry. Oh, yeah. That was damned pretty. Hot. His cock jumped, and Jamie rubbed, trying to get whatever friction he could get. They scooted together, Mel's hand wrapping around his cock, their kiss opening up to let his prick between their lips.

"Oh, God." All he could do was lie there and let them love on him. Brett took the tip right in, sucking down the shaft of his cock, and he thought he might scream.

Mel's lips slid down, down, right to the base of his cock. Then one of his balls was taken into that hot mouth, Mel rolling his nut.

"Mnuhhh." He couldn't even tell them how good it felt. His head rolled back and forth, his hands didn't know where to land, and Jamie knew he was just so fucked. He'd never be able to walk away a second time.

They loved on him, Mel's hands cupping his ass, Brett spreading his legs, everything just so goddamn good. Growling, Jamie pushed up into Brett's mouth, demanding more. He got it, too, Brett sucking him hard, eyes closed, lips sealing tight. Mel licked behind his balls, and then moved to nibble at his sacs, at his inner thighs.

"Please. Brett. Mel... Oh, God." His muscles clenched up, his belly and thighs like rocks. It wouldn't take much. Nothing at all to push him over.

Mel's fingers pushed at his balls, rolling them just so, electricity shooting up his spine.

"Shit!" His whole body shook when he came, the top of his head like to flying off. His cock pushed all the way to the back of Brett's throat, and the man swallowed around him, taking everything in.

When the world came back, Mel was leaning against his legs, lips fastened to Brett's, the kiss wild and hungry.

Shaking off the last of the shivers, Jay scrambled up, his hands finally remembering to move. He pressed between them just enough to touch Brett's cock, his knuckles brushing Mel's wet heat.

The little, raw sounds made him want to howl, made him bare his teeth and touch more.

Brett broke the kiss with Mel, gasping, staring at him. "Come on, baby. Help out here."

Mel reached for him, fingers sliding through his hair. "Jay-love."

"Mel." He kissed her, leaning, hoping he wasn't squishing anyone. He had this whole who do I touch thing going on, but he finally settled for stroking Brett.

Someone's hand landed on his hip, and Mel opened up for him, letting him taste all he wanted. His hips started moving again, his cock trying to perk up, and Jamie kissed Mel deep, pushing in with his tongue. Brett pressed against him, sliding around behind him to push at his ass.

Mel scooted close, so warm, skin soft and smooth where she rubbed against him. "Want you, Jay."

"Yeah? Okay. You got me, honey." He could so do that. So, so do that. He teased Brett a little, wiggling, before pushing Mel down beneath him.

He leaned down, scenting her jaw, her soft, blonde hair, lips tugging at her ear. Mel's leg slid up alongside him, even as Brett's chest warmed up his back.

His cock nudged her wet folds even as Brett's prick pushed along his crease. Moaning, Jay slid inside, trying to be gentle, knowing he just couldn't.

"Mmm." Mel took him so easy, hips rolling to meet him and let him slide home. "Oh, my boys..."

"Missed you so much." His hands found her hips, pulling her up. Brett rubbed and rubbed, finally pushing in, making him cry out.

Mel's hands cupped his face, her body tightening around him.

"Honey... Oh." Staring right into her eyes, Jamie started moving, letting Brett push him forward, slamming back against those lean hips on the way out.

It was easy, to find their rhythm again, Mel rocking up, Brett pushing in. Her hands were everywhere, pinching her nipples, stroking his belly, reaching for Brett.

Brett braced behind him on one hand, the other sliding around to help Mel drive him crazy. Brett touched his belly and chest, then found the spot where he and Mel came together, rubbing just above.

Every time they moved together, Brett's hand nudged Mel and she gasped, squeezing him.

"Oh, Christ." His head was gonna pop right off, with the sparks that shot up his spine. Jamie bent and took a kiss from Mel, gasping into her mouth, begging for more with his whole body.

Mel's tongue fucked his lips, stole his breath and drove him out of his mind. Brett bit into the skin of his shoulder, making him grunt, his hips snapping forward. Oh, God. He was... He was gonna short out.

They had him -- both of them all around him and in him and needing him. It was so fucking huge that he couldn't hold it in. Jamie cried out, his head slamming back against Brett's shoulder, his hips driving his cock into Mel's body. He came again, when he hadn't thought he could so soon, his cock jerking madly.

"So... so fucking fine." Mel was shuddering under him, eyes glowing, hips moving restlessly.

Brett kept thrusting behind him, kept on touching Mel, pushing against her clit with rough fingers. Jay hung there, caught between them, loving their skin and their heat.

"Y'all." Mel's fingers dug into his shoulders, nails stinging just a little. "I. Oh."

He did love that look -- a little lost, a little wild, all woman.

"Come on, baby," Brett growled, chin on his shoulder. "Come on. Show Jay-bird what you got, huh?"

She lurched up, kissed Brett hard, then took his lips, shaking and calling out as she went over the edge.

Brett grunted behind him, biting down on his skin, teeth set hard as Brett filled him with wet heat. Goddamn, they were gonna kill him.

They all slumped down into the mattress, all of them panting, touching.

"Much better than thinking, huh?" Jamie hummed, wrapping around both of them as best he could.

"Mmmhmm. I could just stay right here, forever."

"Yeah." Grinning, Jay kissed Mel's lips, leaning hard. He could stay just like that. Too bad it wasn't gonna happen.

In fact, he heard Brett's stomach growling but good, Mel chuckling at the sound. "Who's cooking breakfast while I..." She stopped, tilted her head. "Somebody's coming up the road."

They all went on red alert, Brett rolling away from him, Jay lifting up off Mel to head to a window.

Mel slid off the bed and snagged a shotgun from beside the door, heading into the front room stark assed naked.

"Man, it'll suck if we have to do this with no clothes." Brett winked from across the room, staking out the back of the house.

"No shit." It was an old truck, an old man driving it.

"It's my neighbor. Y'all stay put." Mel came back in, throwing on some jeans and a t-shirt, a jacket.

Jay growled, not wanting to let Mel go up against even a supposedly friendly neighbor alone.

"If it's a friendly neighbor, why's she taking the shotgun, Jay?" Brett was growling a little himself.

"I don't know." Grabbing his sweats, Jay headed out, making for the back door. He'd just slide around and keep an eye on things where his claws wouldn't gouge wood if he had to change.

The old man had slid out of the truck and was leaning against the fence. "...couple of ne'er-do-wells wandering around on foot, ma'am. The missus asked me to drop in, make sure you was safe."

"Thank you, sir, but I'm doing fine. What happened to your arm, Jasper? Looks like you got bit..."

Shit. Shit. If someone was taking out the neighbors...

"It ain't no big thing, ma'am. I just... You be careful, huh? You're all alone out here."

"I'll be fine, Jasper. Thanks." Mel started back-pedaling, whistling for that big old dog of hers. "You take care, sir."

"Yeah. Yeah, you, too."

The old truck rumbled to life seconds later, and Jay slipped back inside, meeting Brett in the kitchen. "They're taking the neighbors."

Brett nodded. "Yeah. I figured."

"I'm going to feed." Mel was vibrating -- he could see it from there, smell the sour mixture of fury and fear.

"Let me come with you," Brett said, grabbing her upper arms and dragging her up for a kiss.

"I." Her eyes were rolling a little. "I'm fine. Not going to let them take my land. Y'all... Y'all don't have to stand and fight, you don't want to."

Brett shook her even as Jay growled. "Of course we do," Brett said. "We need to do this, Melon."

"What do they want?" She chewed on her bottom lip, bouncing on her toes. All of the sudden Jay noticed she had flipflops on, not boots. Her feet were going to get tore up in the barn.

"You should put your boots on." He kinda fixated on her feet, not willing to think too much on why someone wanted them all dead.

"I know. I want to know who's hunting us. I want to know why. We gave everything up. Everything. All of us. Who'd bother hunting us now?"

"That's what we have to find out." Brett kissed her again, hard enough to make her blink. Oral bastard.

"You... You can't just kiss me and derail me." Brett grabbed her, mouth slamming on hers again. Uh-huh. Brett absolutely couldn't do that...

He was really good at it, in fact. Shedding his sweats, Jamie joined them, kissing along the back of Brett's neck. Brett felt like a brick shithouse against him, solid and muscular and rock-hard. God, he loved the way that man moved, the way each hard muscle flexed. He loved how soft Mel felt when he reached around, too, stroking her hip where her jeans rode low.

She was fighting Brett -- just enough to make Brett growl and push harder, just enough to make Mel need, he knew. Brett bit at Mel's lip, and Jay smelled blood. It maddened him a little, made him growl and rub and bite some himself, the smell of musk heavy in the air.

"Fucker." Mel snarled, snapping at Brett, and fuck, that was hot, the way they went at each other.

They all shifted, Brett lunging, taking Mel right down to the floor, teeth on her throat.

Her nails scraped all along Brett's back as she fought, refusing to go easy. Jay circled around them, touching wherever he could, licking at exposed skin. Fuck they were hot. Mel's eyes flashed up to him, so bright, so fine. That gave Brett the opening he needed, Mel's chin lifted, throat bared for that mouth.

Latching on, Brett sucked hard, biting, and Jay could see Mel arch, her whole body like a live wire. Jamie dove at Brett, snarling, his need to be the big male suddenly rising up. He and Brett went rolling, thumping hard on the floor, his back slamming on the tile.

His fingers scrabbled at Brett's arms, but he just wasn't strong enough. Not against Brett. Goddamn.

Mel slid up, sitting with her back against the wall, just cackling. "Y'all are such boys."

"Shut up," Jay growled, squeaking when Brett bit down on his throat.

"Make me. I can still kick both your asses." She was fucking laughing at them.

They moved as one, both of them rolling toward Mel, grabbing her legs and pulling her down on the floor to pounce on her. He kissed. Brett tickled.

Mel wiggled furiously, trying her best to tickle back, but they had her. They had her in their hands. Brett was blowing raspberries against Melon's neck, and Jay got the backs of her knees. Lord, that girl could shout.

"Y'all!" That laughter rang out, happy and good as all get out.

"Mmm. Hey, Melon." Brett chuckled, rubbing against them both. "We need to get your work done, huh?"

"Yeah." She kissed them, one after the other. "I need to feed and get my shit together 'fore bad things start happening."

"We can actually help," Jay said, patting her ass. "All we need is those clothes you got us. Get your boots, honey."

Mel nodded, sighed a little. "Yep. Feeding before that storm hits. I can smell it in the air."

"Come on, then." They'd worry about the neighbor when the work got done. Hell, maybe they'd all have time to think about who might be doing this if they slowed down a little.

If nothing else, it would make Mel happy for him and Brett to help out. That was incentive enough for him.

***

Brett mucked stalls, thinking how hilarious it was when werewolves owned animals. Really, who in his right mind would have a horse or something that was supposed to be totally afraid of him.

If that damned gelding kicked at him one more time...

Sighing, he moved to water the damned fool animal, hoping to stay out of the way of those big teeth.

"What in hell possessed you to get so many critters, Melon?"

"I needed something to do. I'm not suited to working at the WalMart." No. No, he remembered Mel's temper, how fierce she was. Even walking away from everyone she'd ever fucking known, she'd been defiant as hell.

"You wanted a place to settle, too, huh?" He knew that about her, too. Knew that while he and Jay could wander forever, she was territorial.

"Yeah. I don't change, you know? Unless I have to. I needed a place with a solid attic, with a door that locks."

"Yeah." He needed a place to run, places to hide out, and lots of running water. They'd have to compromise once this was over.

Jamie looked over, shook his head. "We're not human, Mel. You remember that."

"Fuck you, Jay. I always remember. I know. I'm just trying to keep my head down."

"We all have been." Jamie shook his head. "So much good it did us, huh?"

"I don't know, y'all. We're still here." She pushed her hair back when one of the horses reached out his neck to nibble on it.

"Yeah." Brett nodded, grinning a little. "We're back together, too. I see this as a case of unrelenting improvement."

"Yeah. Yeah, I. It was like a bad fucking dream or something." She shrugged, headed for the sweet feed.

"Wait. When we came back, or before?" Jamie followed her, grinning like a fool, and Brett had to laugh.

"Butthead." She spun around, pushing right up against Jay, meeting his eyes. "I wanted y'all. You know that."

"I know, Melon." Jay kissed her mouth, holding her close, and Brett fought the urge to growl about it. They'd proven more than once that he was smack in the middle of them.

Of course, with Jay it was moaning and melting. With him it was a smack and a snarl and then pure fire.

Mmm. Smacking.

Brett stormed over to grab Jay's ass, hands clenching hard as his mouth settled against Jay's neck, teeth biting down hard. Jay yelped and Mel pounced, challenging him over Jay, pushing him.

Oh, he did love a growly Mel. Brett pushed, smooshing Jay between them, his hands landing on Mel's arms. She grabbed a hold of him, kissing Jay so hard the guy's knees buckled. Hell, yes. He bit at Jay's ear, and then licked to ease the sting, pushing against that sweet ass. God, they drove him crazy.

"My boys." Mel's mouth brushed against his, right were it met Jay's skin.

"Yours." Oh, yeah, they were hers as much as Jay and Mel were his. Brett let their scent wash over him, surging up over Jay's back to hump, to bite at Mel.

Mel pulled away, teasing, eyes just damn near glowing. "Come up to the house. The hay'll chafe y'all in tender places."

"Hell, yes. That mean we've done enough work?" He wasn't against hard work at all. No, sir. He'd much rather fuck, though. Then eat. He could murder a hamburger.

"I think we've got some heavy duty touching to work on. I've been working for years." Look at that girl grin. "I was fixin' to revert back to simpering virgin and shit."

"Yeah, like you were any good at that the first time," Jay said, scampering away when they both would have popped him.

"If I remember correctly, neither one of you wanted that until I was about to give it to Bobby."

"Bobby didn't deserve you." That still made Brett about as angry as he'd ever been about anything. "Last one to the house has to make supper."

"Well, then. I want a shower. Don't forget to close the barn doors." Then that little shit girl took off like a shot.

Jay almost made it out before he did, but he grabbed the back of Jamie's jeans and slid past, laughing and running flat out.

Mel could run, sliding on the grass and damn near pole vaulting over the fence. He could feel Jamie breathing down his neck, right at his heels, and Brett put on a burst of speed. No way was he cooking. He'd burn it all.

He almost caught up to Mel, but she slipped in the door, heading down the hall.

Oh. He was gonna catch that ass and tear it up. Skidding, he turned the corner, Jay scrabbling at him from behind. He caught her in the bedroom, whipping her around as she reached for the bathroom door.

"Gotcha!" They tumbled when she knocked his leg out from under him, and Jay landed on them a second later.

"Jesus, y'all are heavy." She was laughing so hard she couldn't catch her breath.

"Jay. Blame Jay."

Ow. Man, Jamie could bite. Those teeth were sharp.

"Jay's got a skinny butt; you're the big boy." Her hand wiggled down to tickle him back.

"Am not." He was, but that wasn't no never mind. It was always Jay's fault. Jay laughed in his ear, wiggling around to kiss him, and Brett figured he'd happily take the blame for that.

Mel pushed into the kiss, her hands sliding up his belly, Jay's. She took what she wanted, and he loved that. Goddamn, her hands felt good. They weren't soft, girly hands, but they rocked his world.

She loved them, too, he could feel it in the way she wrapped those callused fingers around his cock, sliding the fingertips over his slit.

"Melon..." He groaned it out, his hips rising and falling.

"Oh, God, look at you." Jay licked at them both, whatever skin the man could get to, adding to the heat.

"Y'all..." Those hands kept moving, kept driving him crazy.

"Mel. Jay." All he could do was twist to get more, letting them both have his skin, his body.

Mel turned, lips sliding down his belly, nibbling on her way to his cock. Brett moved back to give her more room, and ended up standing, hauling Jay up and around, too, holding him tight against his side. He wanted some of those amazing kisses. Jay's cock nudged against his and Mel took both of them in hand, lips and tongue brushing against them both.

Jay moaned, clutching at him, hands hard and desperate. He took Jay's mouth in a deep kiss, fucking that hot mouth with his tongue, his own hand sliding into Mel's hair.

She managed to get both of them in her mouth, rubbing together, rocking together.

"Fuck." Jay said it against his mouth, body going tight, shaking. Brett nodded, petting his girl, letting her know how good it was.

Those pretty eyes looked up at them, hot as a tin roof in August. Hell, almost as hot as her tongue.

"Sweet, Mel. So sweet." Brett reached down to help, pulling his cock together with Jay's, pressing them tight.

"Mmmhmm." She got her lips around them, the suction starting, pulling them both into her mouth.

They both watched her for a long moment, both of them stunned at how good she felt. Then Brett took Jay's mouth again, chewing on that soft lower lip.

They found themselves a rhythm, in and out, nice and easy so they didn't hurt her, didn't push her too far. Not that he didn't want to jut go for it, but he and Jay were always better than the sum of their parts. Jay started touching him, his hip and thigh, before rubbing along Mel's cheek.

Mel's fingers were around their shafts, holding them together, rubbing as she sucked, head bobbing, hair falling all around them. The whole thing had him going up on tiptoe, moaning loud. It had Jay babbling, telling Mel how fucking pretty she was, how damned fine.

He was going out of his mind, those hands and lips on him, Mel and Jay both moaning, pressing against him. It didn't take long at all before he was roaring to the finish line, his hips snapping, Jay holding on to him so he didn't go too far. Brett howled with it, his head falling back.

Mel moaned, licking at him, taking him in, her smooth skin so hot against him.

"Oh, fuck." He said it against Jay's mouth, all of the aftershocks of his orgasm shaking him. Those two...

"Uh-huh. Mel. Baby. Please." Jay was vibrating.

"Greedy boys." Mel laughed, licking at Jay's belly.

"I'll help, baby." He grabbed Jay's cock, rubbing it against Mel's lips, jacking it slowly. Jay shivered for him, leaning hard.

Mel opened up, let him feed her that long, heavy cock, red, swollen lips wrapped around the shaft.

Jay cried out, body bending back. "Close. So close, y'all."

Mel took Jay down to the root, fingers brushing Brett's fingers, so fucking hot.

Jay came for them, a shout echoing in the room, his cock pushing into Mel's mouth. Brett held him, kept him upright when those knees buckled.

Mel rested between them, forehead on his thigh, just panting.

"How's Melon?" He stroked her hair, fingers combing out a few tangles. "What do you need, baby?"

"Y'all. Y'all, please." She leaned right into his touch, skin hot against his hand.

Sinking to his knees, Brett pulled Jay down, letting Jamie kiss Mel into a puddle. His hand worked between her legs, his fingers finding her center. Wet. So hot, so wet. She moaned into Jay's lips, hips bucking against his hands.

"Mel." Two of his fingers slipped right inside her, opening her up. She took him easily, spreading for him.

"Uh-huh." Fuck, look at her, heart pounding, lips parted for them.

Jay kissed her hard, the wet sound their lips made erotic as hell. Brett rubbed his thumb against Mel's clit, wanting to make her as crazy as she'd made them. Those hips started moving in tiny jerks, circling, rocking against his touch.

"I got you, baby. Come on. Show us what you need."

Jay moaned and nodded, kissing Mel harder, his hands finding her breasts.

"I. I. Oh." Her body arched, belly going tight as she slipped, so wet on his fingers.

God, she was like a firecracker on the Fourth of July. Hotter than anything. He and Jay worked her harder, pushing Mel to her limit. There was nothing prettier than Mel when she came, moaning and rocking, pushing hard against his hand.

"God, I love it when you do that," Jay said, a wealth of satisfaction in his voice. Brett just laughed, biting a little at both of them, smoothing Mel's moisture against her skin.

"Oh, y'all." Mel was all baby-headed, blinking and grinning at them.

"Uh-huh." Breathing them in, Brett smiled back, feeling settled in his gut, feeling like he was home.

He didn't reckon it would last, but he'd take it. He surely would.

***

She got the last glass washed, humming under her breath. Jay made a decent damn pasta. A little messy and a lot heavy on the whole pots and pans usage thing, but it tasted good. The boys were hunting cards and poker chips -- strip poker looked like the game of the evening. Assholes. Beautiful fucking assholes.

"If I made coffee, would y'all drink some?"

"Sure." Brett grinned at her, giving her a drive-by smooch on the way to the hall closet.

"I'll just have that Irish creamer..." Jay added, voice muffled by the couch skirt, where he was digging like a terrier.

"What are y'all doing?" She got to laughing, setting the coffeemaker up to perk.

"Looking for the damned chips. They're not in the linen closet." Jay came up covered with dust bunnies.

"Dude. I need to vacuum. They're in the entertainment center maybe?"

"Okay. We'll check there." They went like a pair of puppies sharing a bone, and if they'd had their tails they'd be wagging.

She pulled out coffee cups, the Irish cream stuff and the sugar, fixing all the mugs up.

"Ha!" Brett held the chips up over his head, letting Jay try to grab them. Lord. Boys.

"Jackasses." She laughed hard, doing her best not to spill the coffee.

"Come play with us, lady," Brett said, heading to the card table. They'd played a hell of a lot of poker back in the day, and Brett was always the impatient one.

"Y'all sure you shouldn't put more clothes on?"

They glanced at each other, shrugging in unison.

"Nah." Jay raised a brow. "We're a little better at this than you."

"Oh, so you think." Jesus. Men. They always assumed she didn't know her ass from a hole in the ground when...

Wait.

What the hell was that?

She spun on her hell and headed for the back-door, grabbing her shotgun on the way. Her nerves were firing like crazy, ears damn near twitching. She heard a low growl behind her, the sound of Brett going into fight or flight mode unmistakable, even after all these years. Jamie was slower, and she could almost sense him scenting the air.

Mel cracked the door, the scent of fear and blood flooding her nose and Frannie stumbled in, bleeding and scared, whining softly in pain. Oh. Oh, you fuckers.

"God damn mother fuckers!" She wrenched the door open, storming out.

Jay barked, the sound ringing out loud, warning her to wait, but she ignored him. Brett went streaking by, a blur of fur and teeth. She pumped the shotgun, eyes adjusting to the dark as she headed down the stairs. Her Frannie. Her dear girl. She smelled smoke and growled, running for the barn. No.

No.

"Shit!" Jamie's human voice sounded next to her, his feet making tracks, heading toward the barn. Somewhere off in the distance Brett was barking, fucking snarling.

She heard the gunfire starting, heard her horses screaming. Jesus Christ. She saw movement to her left and fired, someone screaming as he fell, the butt of the shotgun slamming into her shoulder hard enough to bruise.

Everything went to hell from there, and she lost track of her boys. Another dark shape hurtled toward her, looking like something out of a nightmare, like a bad B movie version of what she was.

She got another shot off before something hit her from the side, knocking her off her feet and slamming her into the ground. Her head bounced hard enough that the moonlight dimmed, went bright red and bloody.

She felt the teeth sting as the sank into her shoulder, and she scrabbled for her gun, fingers sliding over the dust. Before she could blink, whatever it was rolled away under Jamie's bulk, the sound of flesh tearing and screaming sounding like something out of a horror movie.

She shifted, screaming with a pure fury, lashing out at anything that got in her way. Her home, her land. Hers.

That was when the barn went up in flames, the whole roof blazing away like a bizarre bonfire. She stopped, stared, her howl of fury filling the air before she charged toward the flames.

Something cut her off at the knees, but it was Brett, not one of the nightmare things. When she fought him, he took her down again. She snapped, scrabbling at the dirt, shoulder screaming, heart slamming in her chest. Off. Off. She had to. Off.

"Melody, stop." Jamie caught her, holding her still. "You can't go in there now."

"No. My babies." She looked into Jay's eyes, about ready to just scream. "Let me go. I have to help them."

"Brett tried, before... What the hell were those things?"

Brett had tried. Maybe some of her critters were safe. Maybe they. God.

She smelled Frannie, spinning so she could run to the porch, her girl laid out, barely breathing, blood staining everything.

Hunt them.

She was going to hunt them all down and make them pay.

Brett followed, nose on the back of her leg, cold enough to make her shiver. He was limping, but he'd heal up. Jamie was right there, too, scratched and naked and mad as hell. She'd hunt them to hell and back, and she'd have help.

Frannie whimpered and she looked down, staring into those big brown eyes that were starting to glaze.

"I got you. I got you. You're a good girl." She gathered Frannie close, calling softly. "I got you."

Jamie crawled over next to her, hand on her back, his eyes glinting in the dark. He didn't say anything, though, didn't disturb poor Frannie.

She pressed her hand against the torn throat, supporting the poor skin, easing Frannie's way. When the last beat of blood ebbed from Frannie, she eased her onto the porch and stood, heading for the house. She'd get her some clothes and her ammo and then she'd ride.

"I'm sorry, baby." Brett was there next to her, human again, looking beat up as fuck.

"Yeah. There's bandages and shit in the bathroom. Get Jay to patch you." She could feel a tear in her shoulder, leaking down her back, but she didn't give a shit. She left the boys behind, snagging her Levis and her boots, forgoing a bra for a couple of thick shirts and a flannel that'd hold ammo. She grabbed her Bowie, her little pocketknife and the .45 she kept in her underwear drawer.

When she turned around, both of the guys stood in her bedroom doorway, watching her intently.

"Whut?" She couldn't talk to them, not now. She couldn't let them in because, sure as shit, she'd start crying.

"Nothing, honey." Jay just nodded and pulled Brett off toward the bathroom, just like she'd said to.

She grabbed her hat and headed out, nostrils flaring. Her shotgun was out there and she needed to figure out what the hell was what. What was attacking them. How many of her critters got free. How to control her barn fire.

She did okay getting down the steps of the porch, even if her boots did slip on Frannie's blood. She got her shotgun fetched marched toward the big bonfire that was her life. There were lumps on the ground -- masses of something that looked like one of them caught halfway between wolf and man.

She frowned, stared. Jesus. That looked a lot like Harry Balls' boy, Christian.

No.

No, it couldn't be.

Mel grabbed hold of the dead thing, started dragging it toward the fire, just pissed as hell as her shoulder started leaking through her shirts.

Motherfuckers.

Whoever the hell they were, they were going to fucking pay.

They'd killed four of them damned mutated things -- she'd never seen nothing like that before and she didn't give a shit if she did again. There was one still moving, on the east side of the barn, and she pulled her pistol before she got close enough to look.

Familar old blue eyes stared at her. "I warned you, honey. I told you to be careful."

The words sounded like mush in that elongated muzzle, those cracked and crookedy teeth.

"Jasper." Her gorge rose and she stared. "What..."

She reached out and he snapped at her, whimpering at the move. "Don't. I can't. I want to hurt you, honey. So bad."

"Why? What happened to you?"

"Don't know. Happened to us all, honey. You gotta run. We just keep coming and coming."

Tears were streaming down her face. They'd

been good to her. They'd shared hay; firewood. Hell, there were a dozen jars of pickles from them in her pantry. Mel cocked the hammer, stepped hard on the clawed hands that were reaching for her so she could aim.

"I'm real sorry, mister. I swear I am."

She didn't get an answer but a growl, and the report was sharp and loud, wet, warm blood spraying back on her jeans.

Then she started dragging him to the barn fire. She heard the sound of running feet, and before she made it to the fire she had Jay and Brett, both fully clothed now, both carrying guns.

"What was that, baby?"

"It was Jasper. They're my neighbors, all of 'em. I put him down. Get out of my way." She got Jasper's body moving again.

"I'm not in your way." Brett moved to help her, taking part of the weight.

"Don't. Don't help me. I can do it." She couldn't stop the tears, they just kept coming, dripping down her cheeks like the blood sliding down her fingers.

"You can, but you don't have to do it alone." Jay moved in on the other side.

"He was a good man." She tripped in something slimy, scrambling to catch her footing.

"I'm sure he was, baby." There was nothing patronizing there, just low, calm agreement. Brett was good at that shit.

They got Jasper in the fire and she turned away from the light, hunting for more, looking to see what she could. There was nothing out there but the night. The dark. The goddamned unknown.

Okay. Okay, she needed to deal with Frannie.

She stamped around the perimeter of the barn, making sure the grass didn't go. She could hear horses running in the back forty. The boys helped silently, bringing water, trying to help contain the fire. Jay hauled more bodies, the smell of burning flesh almost more than she could stand.

Finally she went to the shed and found her a shovel, heading for the plot beyond the garden.

"Jay, go and see if you can round up the horses. You were always better at it than me." Brett moved out of her way carefully. "I'll keep working on the barn."

She nodded and went to do her job -- digging and crying, working until her palms were blistered and the sky was getting light. They finally buried Frannie, the boys helping without saying a word. Every so often one of them would touch her shoulder.

It was daylight when it was over and she dropped the shovel where it was, headed into the house without a word. They followed her, just like the pair of pups she'd compared them to all those hours ago, solemn and silent.

She locked the door behind them and stepped out of her boots there in the mudroom, setting her shotgun beside the door. She kept her knives and her pistol with her, all the way to the bathroom. That was when they surrounded her, not letting her get away from them now that it was all over. Brett started the shower, Jay started stripping her down.

The shirts were stuck to her wound and she winced as he started pulling them away.

"Shit, honey." Lightly touching the edges of her wound, Jay pulled gently, and then went to get a wet towel.

She looked over at Brett, just staring at him, standing under the water. She couldn't think anymore. Not anymore.

Brett pulled off his filthy clothes and stepped into the tub with her, Jay following seconds later. Jay eased her soaking wet shirts off, popping the wet towel down before the spray could hit her. They took care of her without making a fuss, just letting her lift her face to the spray and wash as much of it as she could away.

The tears kept coming and coming, but no one could see, not with the shower.

Jay and Brett moved in even closer, one in front, one in back, holding her. Nothing but support and soap. It hurt, but it wasn't the worse hurt she'd ever known and she'd survived that. When the water started getting cool, they moved her, drying her, keeping her upright and between them until they landed on the bed.

"I don't think I can sleep."

"We don't have to."

Brett nodded, giving Jay a look. Then the man kissed her gently, sweetly, lips sliding across hers, searching out her tears.

"I'm so fucking mad, y'all."

"I'm sorry, honey. I am," Jay said against her throat. "You have so much more to lose."

"I want to..." She stretched, shaking good and hard.

"Yes." Brett's voice was full of rage and certainty. "We're going to find whoever did this and kill them. For you. You and Billy."

"Yes. I want them to pay. I want them to bleed." She wanted them to hurt like her sweet Frannie.

"We'll make them." Unshakable once he made up his mind, that was her Brett.

She nodded and reached back for Brett's hand. Brett held on, fingers tight and sure around hers. Jay gave her sweet kisses, always wanting to reassure, to soothe. Her body couldn't decide whether to move or stay still, whether to touch or pull away. Her fucking nerves were firing so bad that she was surprised she didn't have a tail.

"Shhh." Nuzzling in, Jay licked just under her jaw, scented her with one cheek. "Breathe, honey."

Her laugh sounded wild as all hell. "I cain't remember how, Jay."

"Sure you can. Suck and blow." His low chuckle made her own laughter mellow out.

"You boys. Always about the sucking and blowing."

"You know it." Brett kissed her cheek. "It's genetic."

She nodded, leaning hard, eyes dropping closed.

"We'll figure it, honey. I promise." Moving so they flanked her, Brett and Jay snuggled up, leaving her feeling safe, at least for a minute.

"I'll hold you to that." She couldn't stay awake, not another second.

"Sleep, baby." Brett whispered it against her ear. "I'll keep watch. Just sleep."

Chapter Three

Pacing back and forth, Brett growled. He'd left Jay snuggled up with Mel in bed, doing his worry stone imitation, and Brett was watching the bright sun shine, watching the embers of the barn burn out.

Goddamn it. As soon as it was dark... He had a feeling they were in for it again.

He was going to just scream with it. If he thought for one minute they wouldn't have come for her, too, if he though he'd brought this on her...

Warm hands landed on his shoulders, Jamie solid as fuck behind him. "She keeps fucking crying in her sleep."

"I'm going to kill whoever this is, Jay." Brett let himself lean. Just for a moment.

"We are. They were coming for her next, Brett. You know that. They were setting her up."

"I know. What the fuck do they want, Jay?" He could see coming after one of them. Maybe him and Jay, if someone was looking for the alpha male types. But Billy? Mel?

"It's the ones that left. All of us." That had been a dark fucking day -- the lot of them so young, so scared. Running because Mel'd refused the Alpha, had slashed the hell out of him, taken an eye, and refused to stand punishment.

Hell, they'd mostly all run with her, knowing that the shit was going to hit the fan.

"I get that. I just don't know why. Who? Lance has to be dead by now." Lance had been a hellacious bad-ass of an alpha. Brett had wanted to kill him more than once.

"I don't know. If it was about Mel, why not just take her?" Jay leaned a little harder. "Shit, Brett. If it was about her, why didn't they come in blazing?

They weren't trying to kill her."

"I know." Thank God. They would have been completely unprepared if someone had come in any harder than they had. "We have until dark, I think."

"You want to run?"

"Mel won't. Not until she has to. This is her place." He turned, wrapping his arms around Jamie and holding on tight, lips finding the pulse that beat too fast at the base of Jay's throat.

Jamie kissed his temple and stepped close. "I'm not ready to die, man. I'm no fucking coward, but we're sitting ducks here."

"I hear you. Our best bet may be to start tracing their steps back." If that made any sense. Brett breathed deep, smelling Jamie, needing the closeness, the touching.

"Mmmhmm." Jamie's hand slid down his back, stroking good and hard, nails almost like claws.

His spine arched, his whole body pushing into the touch. "Jay..."

"I got you." Jay did. Jay wanted him, too, cock hard against his hip.

Brett grabbed the back of Jay's head, sinking his hands into thick hair before taking a hard kiss, his rage channeling into need. Jay opened right up, tongue pushing into his lips, fucking his mouth.

That was it. Just that. He wrapped one leg up around Jay's hip, rubbing them together. Suddenly he was hard as nails.

Jay growled, body responding immediately, ferally. The 'yes' and 'please' and 'now' where right on the air.

He took Jay down, right down on the floor, covering that solid body with his. He humped, needing friction, biting Jay's shoulder. Jay snarled, pushing up, bumping into him good and hard, his knees leaving the floor.

"Come on, Jamie. Give it to me." The words would have been incomprehensible to anyone who wasn't half wolf, but he knew Jamie heard him. Felt it in the bite on his upper arm.

Spunk sprayed on his belly, his cock, marking him, hot as hell. He growled, biting back a howl so he didn't wake Melon. He came like a ton of bricks, though, pushing against Jay. Marking right back.

Jamie held on tight, tongue sliding over his jaw, tasting him. Low noises came out of him, subvocal, really. Just calling to Jay, telling him that they needed to get safe.

Jay answered, worrying about Mel, about how to move her, get her out of here.

They'd have to. They couldn't stay. They couldn't just wait to die.

The bedroom door opened, Mel looking over at them. The bite on her shoulder looked fucking horrifying - crusted and deep red, swollen. "I'm going to all the neighbors, see who's left."

"Melon." Climbing to his feet, Brett went to her, steering her back toward the bathroom. "No one's left. I can tell you that. It's just like Billy's place."

"That can't be true. They can't all be gone." She was holding onto this shit by the skin of her teeth.

"Mel." Now Jay was with them, getting the antiseptic. "They are. We have to move."

"I'm not leaving my land. I can't. This place is mine. I've worked it, loved it, poured all I am into it."

"Do you want to watch it all burn, Mel? Want to watch it all go down with us in it?"

"Then go. Y'all go and let me be!" She grabbed hold of a toothbrush holder, howling as she smashed it into the mirror, shattering both.

"Stop! Mel, stop. We're not splitting up again!" Brett shook her, his hands clenching so tight on her arms that he heard bones grind.

She stared at him, eyes rolling in their sockets, the wolf just right there under her skin. Maybe that would be the best thing. Maybe the wolf would know what Mel couldn't admit. If she ran her territory... Brett leaned down and bit her. Hard. He heard Jay's snarl, the sound tearing the air as Mel screamed, pulling away from him, claws scoring his skin.

Come on, baby. Come on. Let the wolf out. Brett thought hard of tails and teeth, feeling his body shrink, lower to the ground. Mel growled, that beautiful pale fur right there, soft and thick, eyes glowing for him, teeth bared. Licking her muzzle, he turned to the door, Jay right there like a dark shadow. Time to run.

She was on his tail, moving like a flash, stopping to scent the blood on the back porch. No. No thinking. Only instinct. Jay helped, circling behind her and nipping at her heels. She barked and took off, streaking across the pasture, taking a wide berth around the ruined barn.

Yes. They needed to stay with her, but this was a good sign. Nipping at Jay, Brett ran, flat and low to the ground. They kept her moving, kept her running and running until the scent of death was gone.

Oh, better. Better. Brett knew Mel wouldn't be ready to play, but maybe she was ready to hunt. They needed something. A rabbit.

Mel turned, body sliding against his and he nudged her, scenting her. His pack. Jay barked, pushing into their touch, tongue lolling. Their silly boy. He nipped Jay's ear. She yipped and nuzzled, snuggling Jay between them, panting hard. Jay rumbled happily, wiggling between them. Such an attention whore. It was good, though. Right.

There was a snap of a branch, a crack, and

Mel's hackles rose, teeth bared immediately as she crouched and growled, deep and low. They all turned, growling, spreading out into a hunting formation. No one was going to get them. No one. They moved together, Mel's nose to the ground, nostrils flaring as she sniffed hard.

Suddenly Jay barked, tail waving, and took off running, flushing a rabbit out of the brush. Ask and ye shall receive. They worked easily together, the big jackrabbit making them run for it, making them work.

The taste would be much sweeter if they had to give chase. Barking, Brett took off around in a wide arc, intent on cutting the escape route off. Mel came through the middle, barking and confusing their prey, teeth snapping.

The rabbit squealed and went down as Jay and Mel took its legs. Brett gave a short howl, as proud as he could be of his pack. The best bits were offered to him and he almost howled with the sudden rush of heat and pride and pleasure. He took them gingerly, licking at them, waiting to see how the rest settled out. Mel and Jay shared, Jay nosing over the rest of the organ meat to their girl. Such a fine wolf. Mel lapped it up, then set to grooming, licking and biting at her shoulder.

Better. So much better. They just needed to find a place to sleep off their meal, someplace where when they woke up, they'd have the fucking jump on anyone who came back for Mel's house. Jay came to him, chuffing and muttering, letting him know it was time to move, to sleep. He yipped, licking at Jay's muzzle, nudging him toward the west. Toward the higher ground.

Mel watched them, blinking with tired eyes. Brett pushed at her, nudging her until she growled at him, but she'd go. He knew she would. She got to her feet, snapping and snarling, leaning into his weight. Flanking her, Jay pushed up against her, and they all staggered for a moment. Then Brett barked and turned to lead the way, knowing they needed to get to cover.

His pack followed, moving with him toward the copse of trees, the little hidden den that he'd found on his trip here. There. There they could rest and recover, as they always did better in wolf form. Brett led the way, his tail waving high.

They curled together, Mel's muzzle tucked in his ruff, soft little whimpers sounding. Licking at her, Brett called to Jay, who lay down on her other side, tail across Mel's, little yips sounding. Meant to soothe.

It worked, too, Mel settling between them with a heavy sigh. Yes. Yes, love. Safe. Sleep.

They would stay until nightfall, at least. Yeah. Then they would decide on fight or flight. For now, though, Mel could rest.

That was the most important thing.

***

Jay woke to the smell of burning. It seared his nose, coated his tongue, black and oily and hard.

His ears twitched, the sound of something cracking and breaking making him lift his head. Somewhere off in the distance, he could see a glow on the horizon, the red and yellow and orange startling against the black night.

Shit.

He raised his head, scenting the air. Brett. Mel. Fire. Jamie barked, trying to wake the others. Mel's eyes popped open and she was gone, running hard, streaking away from them.

No. Shit, shit, shit. He growled, snapping at

Brett's ass before taking off after her, flat out running to catch up. Brett's bark was sharp, insistent, and Mel didn't listen one bit, just running and running. Fucking stubborn bitch.

Brett passed him like he was standing still, making him work to keep up. Making it so he got back to Mel's house just in time to see the roof collapse.

Mel headed for the back porch, body slamming against the smoldering back door.

"No!" It came out of his very human throat, his body knowing it would be easier on two feet than on four. "Mel! No!"

Brett grabbed for her as the door popped open, his hands landing on her hind legs. Jamie scramble to help, hands grabbing, pulling at her fur. There wasn't enough left in there to risk anything for. Not that she would admit it. She shifted, skin hot and slick as she fought them, screaming and wild, pure hurt and fury in her howls.

"Oh, honey." It fucking broke his heart, made him want to tear someone limb from limb. Made him want to hit Brett and tell him to make it all better.

"Let me go!" Her paws, hands, whatever, were already blistered.

"No, Mel. I'm not going to lose you." Brett pulled her around, flinging her off the porch like she was a poodle.

Mel landed hard, sprawling in the grass, sobbing as she scrambled to stand. Jay made a leap for her, but Brett got there first, slamming down on top of her to hold her down. Jamie just paced, staring and growling.

"Let me go! You motherfucker! Jamie! Help me!"

"Melon..." He went to her, hands reaching out, stroking her face, her hair. "It's gone, honey."

"No. No. I have to. Please, y'all..." Her poor blistered hands reached for him.

"Oh, honey." Jay held her, tugging her out from Brett's grasp.

Brett growled. "Keep her there. I'll get anything I can." Like a damned flash, Brett was gone, right into the house. Damn him.

She groaned, calling for Brett, so fucking lost. "What the hell is this, Jamie?"

"I don't know. We're gonna find out. We're not going to--" Grunting, he rolled away from Mel, a heavy, wet body landing on his, clawed hands ripping at him.

Mel screamed, turning on the attacker, tearing it off him and attacking with a snarl.

It took two seconds to change, his wolf coming to the fore, his teeth sinking into... whatever that foulness was, ripping at it. Brett came barreling out and things went all fur and blood, the beasts coming from everywhere, snarling.

Their world turned to snarls and claws, tearing and slashing, all of them trying to keep the beasts at bay. It was a fucking nightmare. They ended up together, being driven by this pack of... monsters. Pushing them deeper into the forest, driving them away from the flames.

Even he was smart enough to know that he was being herded. That those assholes could have taken them down at any time. Where in hell were they going? It was Mel that stopped, stood her ground, snapping and snarling and refusing to move.

"Oh, I don't think so, bitch." The words stunned him and they spun, a tall, broad man covered with scars just staring at Mel, snarling. It was like slow-motion, watching one hand raise, a dart flying through the air and burying itself in Mel's neck.

Brett went crazy, running at the guy, teeth bared

in a Wild Kingdom moment if he ever saw one. That tail looked like a flag, Brett ran so fast.

Mel toppled like a tree, landing on her side with a sickening thump, eyes rolled back up in her head. Brett was in mid-leap when he went down, rolling over and over, leaves crackling madly.

The only thing he could do was stand and fight. No way was he going to run; he couldn't leave his pack again. Jamie snarled, crouching, waiting. They'd have to come to him.

"Come now, James. Of all of them, you were the least likely to fight. It's me, don't you remember?"

He tilted his head, trying to place the voice, trying to remember the last time someone called him James. His wolf brain couldn't fathom it, could only hear the challenge. He leaped, ready to rip that scarred throat right out.

He felt the dart hit his skin, the world going dark in a brutal, sudden wave. Golden glowing eyes stared at him, just barely visible. "Tch-tch-tch. I win."

Chapter Four

"Wake up, bitch." The blow spun her around and she stumbled, trying to get her bearings.

It took another two blows before she got them, striking out, hands meeting flesh. "Back off."

What the fuck.

What. The. Fuck.

Hands tangled in her hair, dragging her backward. "Oh, I don't think so. You remember when you left here? You remember turning your Alpha down? You won't get that chance again."

She knew that voice. She knew... "Wayne?"

"Melody. So good of you to remember me, after the way you all ran off and left me." The sneer had gotten better over the years, had become adult somehow.

"We asked you to come." She wasn't going to play bitch for that asshole, she couldn't have, no matter what the punishment was. "Why did you stay?"

"Does it matter now?"

Well, obviously it did or she wouldn't be there. Asshole.

"Well, duh. Where are the boys? Why did you fucking attack everyone? No one was hurting you. No one was fucking involved with you."

"They all had to die. You and your boys, though? You're gonna go slow. I have plans." He slapped her again, the casual brutality of it making her ears ring.

She met that face, the scars across it heavy and brutal. "Fuck you, asshole. You think you can fucking scare me, you ugly coward?"

Jesus. Jesus, this was her fucking fault. They all died because of her.

"I think I will." He laughed, the sound raw and

ugly. "I think I'll start with your precious James."
Wayne snapped his fingers.

It didn't matter what hurt, how badly it burned,
she wouldn't let this go. She leapt, changing, snapping at those fingers, taking three off at the hand.

Wayne screamed, falling back from her, just like
he always did. Two of the weird, shuffling not-wolf
things came at her, dropping Jamie's limp form with
a thud. Then the world exploded, because Jay wasn't
limp anymore, was right there with her, snarling and
snapping.

Motherfucker.

She didn't care about the monsters. She focused
on that fucking murderer. That goddamn coward.

Jamie was calling, barking, trying to find Brett,
one after another of those rotten, walking corpses
falling under his teeth. Fucking Wayne, though, he
ran, backing away, trying to hide from her. She followed, snarling and biting and... Jamie's scream
stopped her. She couldn't let them have her boys.

Mel turned, barking, heading for her Jay. Jamie
was surrounded, but was putting up a damned good
fight, bouncing back and forth, taking out knees and
ankles. Where the fuck was Brett? She snarled, a
white hot rage taking her. Her men. Her home. Her
life.

They took down one after another, flesh tearing,
blood pouring over the floor. A high whistle sounded, and it was like time stopped. They all stared at
each other, and then the half-wolf... things. Well,
they ran. Just flat out left them ready to finish the
fight.

She looked at Jay, barking. Brett. They needed
to find Brett. Now. Jay yipped, turning and started
for the door, picking his way between blood and fur,
nose working double time.

She let him hunt, keeping watch, snarling and

snapping at any tiny movement. The wind made the metal roof and walls shudder and groan. The scent of oil and grease was strong, confusing. Where the fuck were they?

Whining, Jay turned his head back to look at her, nosing toward a door with a padlock and a chain. Yeah. Yeah, okay. With the tear on his flank, there was no way Jamie could shift back to human and open it.

She shifted, swaying, fighting to get to her feet. Her face felt swollen and hot and her shoulder burned like fire, but one of her men was back there and... Okay. Mechanics. This was a mechanic's. Tire iron. They had to have a fucking tire iron.

It took her a few minutes to find an iron bar, and a few more minutes to get it to tangle in the chain. She banged and twisted, screaming with pure frustration as she tried to break them free. Whining, Jamie grabbed at the damned chain with his teeth, pulling, his strength so much bigger than hers. He growled, fighting to get to Brett just as hard as she was.

She looked down into Jamie's eyes, just about ready to cry. This was her fault. Her fucking fault. All she would have had to was spread for the Alpha. Or stay for the punishment for disobedience.

She snarled and pulled hard, something in her hurt shoulder popping and going numb as the chain snapped. She got the door open just in time for Jay's lunge, his furry body hurtling through the opening. The room was inky dark and smelled like blood. Heavy and metallic.

"Brett." She reached for a light switch, hand slapping along the wall until she found it.

Brett was there, and he was alive. She could hear his heartbeat, fast and a little unsteady, but sure. He was naked, human, and cut up from the soles of his feet to his collarbones. Only his face was untouched.

"Brett. Fuck. Wake up. Change." Her one arm wouldn't lift, so she reached for the chains with her left. "Jay. Love. Push him up. Help me."

Low growls came hard and fast, Jay leaping over to help, nudging and pushing. He was healing fast, the gaping wound on his flank closing. Soon he'd be able to shift, to use his hands. Then she could change back and heal her own damned wounds.

Brett grunted when Jay stepped on his legs, eyes flying open.

"Brett. Come on, lover. We need you to help us."

"Mel?" Jesus, his voice was creaky, shot to hell. He shook his head. "Fucking A. You're alive. I need... need to change."

"Well, no shit. Stand up and I'll get you down." Jesus. Get down and change so she could get them moving and free.

"Nah, I'm just gonna lay here, Melon." The usual sarcasm was right there, just like it always was, almost making her grin.

"Get on with it, fuckhead," Jay said, changing slowly, his words growly, not quite human.

"I'm not in the motherfucking mood, guys." She shoved, Brett snarled, Jay yelped and the fucking chains came loose. Then Brett landed on Jay and they both went back to furry, snarling and sniping.

She grabbed the chain, slapped it on the floor, the snap sharp and short, like a gunshot. They both stared at her and she stared back. "Go. Run. Right now. Both of you get out of here."

Brett came over and took her hand between his teeth. The touch was gentle, but the message was clear. Not without her.

She reached out with her left hand, stroked the

long face. "I can't. I can't, y'all. I'm sorry, but you gotta go." She didn't have it in her to run now. She needed to finish up, make amends.

They sat on either side of her, leaning on her legs. Goddamn. They were with her. No matter what.

She panted, needing to change so bad. She slid down to the floor, tears sliding down her face. "Y'all..." God, they were warm.

The wolf came, demanding its time to heal and she leaned, hard. Brett licked her cheek, growling, urging her to change. To heal. Then they would go after Wayne. She could see it as a promise in his eyes.

It was what she needed, so she did. She let go and let the wolf take her. Let her boys have their way a little bit longer.

**

The full moon was almost on them.

In a way, it was a damned good thing. It meant they healed faster, meant they could run for hours and not tire, despite what they'd been through.

The old lady in the sky guided them, kept them going, even when Brett thought they'd collapse. Jay was panting, whining with almost every step, still too damned weak. Melon, well... She was hurting. Not just physically. She was ready to bolt again.

Somehow they were gonna have to break her of that.

When the old house came into view, he barked, turning sharply, running right for it. The place had the smell of decay, of desertion, and Brett knew they could use it to regroup. His pack followed, moving slowly, Mel sliding around the back to check things out.

Jay checked the front porch, and was the first to

change back to human, his body shimmering and shuddering for long moments. Then he limped right up to the door, flinging it open. And people said their Jay was a coward.

Old and dusty -- there hadn't been anyone here in years. It was perfect. He and Jay wandered on the inside -- he found a chest with old linens and another with simple, threadbare clothes. Jay found a mattress that would do, covered up.

Mel they found asleep in the sun on the back porch, whining softly in her sleep and running.

Kneeling next her, his bones creaking like an old man's, Brett shook her gently. His voice felt wrong, unused. "Melon. Come on, baby. Inside."

She opened her eyes, stared at him with this horrible shame, this guilt that made his mouth sour. Then she stood up, padded inside.

Waiting for them in the bedroom, Jay sat cross-legged on the mattress, holding his hands out to them. "Come on, love," he said to Mel. "Come on."

Mel jumped up, landed next to Jay, leaving room for him.

Lord, he was tired. Brett eased himself down, wanting to scream at how tired and beat up they all were. Instead, he settled in next to Mel, hooking an arm around her. Mel slowly came back to herself, fur fading, eyes staying the same, staring at him.

"Melon, stop." Brett stroked her cheek, thumb brushing gently over the bruise he saw there. "This is not your fault."

"It is. It was Wayne. All of them died because of me."

"No." The scratchy growl came from Jay, and Brett made a mental note to check Jay's throat for injuries. "No, it's all Wayne's fault. He's the one who stayed behind and waited for us to get caught."

"And whose fault was it that we had to run? I should have just... I was too fucking proud." No. No, she was theirs. They fucking loved her -- him and Jamie -- and just because that son of a bitch was Alpha, didn't mean he could take all he wanted.

"Whose fault was it?" Jamie rose up on his knees, almost a solid bruise from head to toe. "Fucking Wayne's, that's who. Fuck, Melon, it was when you turned him down that the fucking alpha started looking at you twice. And we asked him to come with us!"

"I ruined fucking everything!" Melody screamed, launching herself across the bed.

It was all he could do to catch her, but Brett managed it, pulling her back until she slammed into his chest. "Melon, stop. Stop." Fighting her, he got her turned around, got his mouth on hers.

Jamie pressed against their sides, holding on as Mel kissed him, the heat sudden and sharp and fierce. Yes. They needed it, no matter how beat to hell they were. They needed to touch, to feel, to be alive. Brett pulled them both to him, holding tight.

Mel reached for Jay, trembling fingers stroking his face, petting him. Jamie moaned, leaning in to kiss her, too, sort of bowling them all over on the bed again. That got them some grunting and groaning, but it didn't matter. They were all touching.

Mel's kisses were sloppy, their lady pulling away and pressing close, like she couldn't figure out where she was. They would make sure she knew. Brett growled, and Jay moved in until they were all three sharing a kiss, lips and tongues moving, Mel pressed tight between them.

There. There, good. He could smell it, smell Mel's need, smell Mel's desire. That's it.

Jay touched her, pushing up under her breast to raise it, offering it to both of their mouths. Brett bent, sucking at Mel's nipple, scraping it with his teeth. Mel's cry sounded good to him and he pulled harder, wanting her to remember that he wasn't going to let her go. Never again.

He knew Jamie felt the same way, could feel it in the way that hard body pushed against his, in the way Jay bit and licked and set to driving Mel crazy. Brett's cock felt like stone, heated to the melting point. Mel moaned, one leg wrapping around his hip, ass pushing back against Jay, slick curls sliding against him.

"Mine." They were his. His cock brushed against Mel's softness, trying to find its place, even as Jay pushed against her from behind. For a moment their cocks brushed against each other before both of them pulled back to try again.

Mel's laugh was just... it made him grin and growl. "Boys."

She eased him over and straddled him. Then she tilted her hips, took him in slow and deep. "Okay, Jay-love. Nice and easy."

His eyes rolled and he whimpered. They'd done this before, taken her together, but not in so long. Brett held his breath, waiting for the slow, torturous glide of Jay pushing in. Jay moaned, moving up, sliding in, all of them freezing for a long moment.

Then Mel moaned, leaned down and kissed him. "Y'all."

"Yes. We're together." He kissed her again and again, Jamie licking at Mel's shoulder, at her neck. He could feel Jay pressing down against him, loving on both of them.

Mel nodded, belly hard as hell against him, hips rocking in the tiniest of motions. They eased her into it, their hands meeting at her waist. Brett pulled and Jay pushed, and soon they were moving faster, just a little harder. Mel groaned, moving with them, loving on them both, holding them both.

His mouth moved on whatever skin he could find, from Mel's chest to Jay's arm. His balls drew up, his breath catching in his chest.

"Brett." She breathed into his mouth, eyes rolling. "Jay. Love. Please."

"Yes. Oh, baby. Yes." Jay reached around and he reached down, both of them working her with their fingers, both of them pushing into her harder and harder.

Jay's cock slid against his, both of them rubbing against Mel's slick, hot walls. She jerked for them, bearing down, squeezing them both tight as she came for them.

"Christ!" Jamie shot hard against him, cock jerking wildly, and Brett cried out, holding on to both of his lovers, unwilling to let go, even when his muscles went weak.

Mel slumped down onto him, moaning softly as she cuddled in.

"I got you, baby." His throat was raw, his voice blown, but he had to tell her. Had to. "I love you, baby."

"Love y'all." Her tears slid onto his shoulder, hot and slick. "Always have. So much."

"We deal with this together, Melon," Brett said, kissing away a tear.

"We go after him and finish it," Jay agreed, leaning past her to kiss him, Jamie's cheek rubbing against Mel's.

"I'm so sorry." She leaned into him even harder, nose rubbing his jaw. "Y'all look so fine. My boys."

"Ours." Jay growled it, licking at them, heavy and hot and pushing Mel down against him.

Brett had to laugh a little, at life, at the circumstances it took to bring them all together again. He couldn't be sorry, though. They'd come full circle, found their way back.

Now all they had to do was fight to keep it.

Chapter Five

They moved through the forest, healed and whole, running fast with the moon on their side.

Wayne and his monsters were close. They needed to find them and take them down. Wayne was hurt, without a pack, vulnerable and they were...

Mel ran around a patch of fallen bois d'arc, the scent of black soil strong in her nose, for the first time in years.

They were back on familiar ground and pissed off.

Brett and Jay moved smoothly, easily, one of them at her side, the other forging ahead. The way they took turns made her tongue loll out with laughter. They weren't letting her out of their sight.

It was Jay that caught the scent, hackles rising, nose wrinkling as his teeth bared. They all stopped, Brett sniffing the ground, nudging them both around so they weren't heading straight in. They needed to be smart about this.

There was another metal building -- industrial and huge, but not well-kept, one of the monsters slavering and slobbering at the front, another around back.

Brett slipped away like smoke, leaving her and Jay to take the front. She wasn't gonna be insulted by the idea that it would take two of them to do what one of Brett could. He had the biggest score to settle as far as the damned beating they'd taken.

Of course, she had the biggest score to settle with Wayne. She'd taken three fingers.

They headed down the hill, going for speed and surprise to take the monster down, Jay going for the flank so she could take the throat. They worked like a team now, both of them getting back into the groove of thinking at the same time. Bones snapped under Jay's strong jaws, the thing screaming for a split second before she silenced it.

They backed away, Jay looking toward the back, ears swiveling. Nothing. No sound. Brett was in. She tossed her head and headed for the front door, staying low as she could. Jay chuffed, the sound low and pleased, rearing up to push the door open, letting her keep watch.

Inside, there was total chaos, Wayne screaming and waving his hands, scarred body uglier in the sunlight. A shadow moved from the back of the big structure, telling her Brett was there, waiting. Ready to move in.

They slid against the walls, circling, surrounding. This was going to be over.

Today.

Jay moved clockwise to her, and soon they had all the danger spots covered, ready for a concerted attack. Part of her wanted to ask Wayne why one more time. Ask what he thought he was doing, where he'd gotten the scars. The other part just wanted to kill him.

"You bitch." Those wild eyes fastened on her, focused on her. "They fucking beat me, made me take all your punishments, you cunt."

She bounced and snarled, daring him to come get her. Make a mistake.

Wayne threw himself at her, hands growing into claws. But he couldn't change. Not all the way. Brett hit on one side, Jamie on the other and she went for the knees. They tore at him, knowing he wasn't right, wasn't ever going to stop coming after them. He was as foul as his creations, sour and soft and odd.

He screamed, beating at her, at her boys and she just kept attacking, the monsters staying back, staying away. Jay leaped, only to be tossed away, and

Brett growled, going right for Wayne's throat. She went for his balls, teeth snapping down hard. The scream was pure, insane terror, pure pain.

Wayne went limp, slumping to the floor, and not five seconds later, every one of the others, the things, went down, too. Falling over on their own steam.

She stumbled back, panting hard, eyes rolling as she snapped at the air.

Staggering, Brett changed from wolf to human, hands reaching out. He stroked her muzzle before going to Wayne and testing his pulse. "I need a god-damned shovel."

She blinked, licking at Brett's fingers, confused. Shovel?

"His head has to come off. I want to be sure." Limping just the tiniest bit in his human form, Brett went hunting, his bruises showing on his human skin.

She concentrated on shifting, forced herself to change. This was her fault, her problem. Jay whined, shimmered, but stayed a wolf. He licked her leg, telling her he wasn't a coward. He wasn't.

Hell, she knew that.

She bent down, cheek sliding against her Jay-Love's muzzle. "Mine. You hear me? I need you, you and Brett."

He licked her cheek before going to sit vigil in front of Wayne, waiting for her and Brett.

Brett slammed doors open on their tracks, searching for something that would do the trick. He swore viciously, getting more and more agitated. He hated to leave things undone.

"Relax, Brett." She got up, started looking, started trying to help.

"I just don't want this to end up like a horror movie, baby." His hand brushed hers when he went by, and he flashed her a grin.

"No. No." She nodded at him. "There's gasoline. Y'all get out of here." She'd watch the motherfucker burn.

"Oh, good idea. We're not going to just walk off and leave you to it, though." Damned stubborn man.

"Stubborn asshole. I need some clothes."

"So do we." Brett patted her ass. "We need to make sure none of them come back."

"I know. I know." Of course, she didn't have the foggiest fucking idea what she was supposed to do after.

"Come on." They started hunting, coming up with some old coveralls and a couple of grungy flannel shirts. Better than nothing. Jay just sat where they left him, staring down at Wayne.

They dumped the clothes on Wayne and she poured the gasoline on, the smell making her gag.

"Go on, Jamie. Guard our exit."

Jay barked, turning and trotting to the door. Every line of his furry body spoke of Jamie's readiness to have this over.

She met Brett's eyes, "I'm sorry, love. I would never have brought this on you." Not in a million years.

"You didn't." Rubbing his hand up and down her arm, he smiled. "We were young. He was crazy. He always was. Help me find something to spark this fire."

"There's one of them propane things. It'll go fast." She hoped.

"It will. Okay. Let's get this show on the road." They dragged canisters over, got the burner set up, and stood looking down at Wayne. At least until Jay barked at them, impatient as hell.

"Damn it, Wayne. It didn't have to be ugly. You could've run." She whimpered a little and then set the fire.

"He could have, but he thought we'd get caught, and he'd look like the good boy." Jamie finally managed the change, standing in the doorway, swaying from the suddenness of having two legs. "He always wanted to be the good one. He was rotten to the core. Don't you feel bad for him."

Brett grimaced, turning his back and walking away. Yeah. Jamie should know. He always took the brunt of Wayne's bullshit.

"Okay." She watched a little longer, until the fire hurt her eyes.

Then she turned and walked away, letting it all burn.

Leaving it behind. Hopefully for the last time.

Epilogue

"Honey, hand me the damned hammer, will you?" Jamie was re-hanging a gutter, of all things. Melon insisted they needed them. He and Brett would just let the rain run down the sides of the cabin...

"Here you go, babycakes," Brett said, climbing up behind him on the ladder and pinching his ass. "Mel went to get something from the barn. Chicken wire. Chicken feet. Something."

"Don't make me beat you both, assholes." Mel was dragging the wire, bowed under the weight -- stubborn bitch. "I got to get them goats and chickens safe before you two change again."

Uh-huh.

Right.

They hadn't eaten that rooster during the last full moon.

Jay hammered the last piece of flashing into place, hanging the gutter on the hook he put in. "Let me down, Brett." He wiggled his ass, just to emphasize his point.

A sharp slap landed on his butt. "Why would I do that, Jay?"

"Because it's hard for us to gang up on Melon when we're on a ladder." His muscles jumped, his cock firming right up from the slap.

"Oh. Excellent point. She's not wearing a bra."

"I know. Now let me down." He pushed back with his butt, and the whole ladder almost went over with them, but Brett moved fast. They landed on the ground and turned on Mel as a unit, both growling a little. Ready.

She squeaked some, the sound happy as hell, just fine. Their girl had lost all that horror, all the pinched, lonely worry on her face. They were slowly but surely healing the old wounds. All they had to do was remind her that she had family. Daily.

Mel watched them, and then bolted for the house, moving like a streak.

Brett shot him a grin and took off. Jay took it as a sign that all of his working out was paying off that he beat Brett to the door by a half inch. They tumbled inside, following Mel to the bedroom, leaping after her when she bounced.

Oh, fuck. She smelled good. Warm. Sweet. Like him and Brett and hay and... He bit down on her hip, making her jerk, making her thighs spread.

"Hey, baby," Brett said, sliding up Mel's body, rubbing all up on him at the same time.

"H...hey." Man, those little button-down shirts just popped buttons like nobody's business.

The jeans were tougher, but Jamie figured he had good hands. He got them open, slid them down Mel's thighs. She had these tiny lace panties -- one of those weird things they'd learned about their tough broad along with her love of popsicles and that her ears were pierced.

Brett always went for the panties, so Jay concentrated on Mel's lack of bra, crawling up to lick at the underside of one breast. Brett pressed against him, hot as fire, even through his clothes. Mel's fingers tangled in his hair, encouraging his mouth to that hard, peaked little nipple, even as Brett's cock rubbed against his ass. Bossy. They were both fucking bossy.

Jay licked, then sucked hard, letting Mel have what she wanted, letting her feel his bristly chin on her soft skin. Oh, she tasted good. The sound of ripping lace made him chuckle, blowing air against her skin.

"Fucker." Mel growled, one hand landing on Brett's skin, the smack sharp and loud.

Brett laughed, the sound pure joy. "Soon, yeah.

Just let me get in position..."

She rolled up, pouncing Brett, the big male's shoulders bouncing on the mattress, her hands holding him down. "You were saying?"

"I can be a fuckee." Those big hands landed on Mel's ass, though, never still.

Jay grunted. "Elbow. Chin. Nice."

"Come here, Jay-love. I'll make it up to you." Mel leaned toward him, pulled him down into a kiss that threatened to set his short-hairs aflame.

"Sorry, lover." Brett shifted to rub his back with one hand, kinda yanking him over against them. Oh, better. Now, if he could just get Mel on Brett, he could move up and get Brett open...

Mel pulled out of the kiss, cheeks flushed, eyes sparkling a little. "Not bad, Jay-love."

"I do try." He grinned back and scrambled around, pressing up against her back. God, she had a pretty ass, so lush and round. Brett wasn't a slouch, either.

"Mmm." Mel pushed back toward him as she leaned down to kiss Brett.

"Sweet." The wet sound of their kiss had him rubbing and moaning, licking salt off Mel's shoulder. His hands found her breasts, lifting them, fingers rolling her nipples. His cock pushed against Brett, against the soft sacs, the tender skin.

"Mmmhmm." Mel groaned, shivering against them. "We got a plan, y'all? I'm wanting."

"I think Jay's got one." Brett's voice had lowered to a growl, those big hands on Mel's hips, his thighs.

"Mmmhmm. Up, Melon." He pushed her up, and then lowered her down on Brett's cock, loving how they both moaned for him.

Mel settled down, and then started moving, sliding up and down Brett's cock, nice and easy. Jay gathered up Mel's moisture, got his fingers good and wet. Then he pushed two inside Brett's body. They'd never been a pair for gentle and sweet, him and Brett. Just getting down to business.

"Oh, honey. Do that again. Look at his eyes." Mel was right there with him.

Growling, he pushed again, staring over her shoulder at Brett. His lovers. His pack.

Brett licked his lips, grinning wildly. "Enough with the niceties, lover. In me."

Mel's laugh rang out and she leaned forward, fingers sliding through Brett's chest hair, heading to tease his nipples. "Pushy man."

"You know it, baby. You feel how hard I am for you two?"

Even Jay could feel that, his free hand pushing where Mel and Brett joined, rubbing insistently. His cock ached, and he got on with it like Brett demanded, sliding his fingers free, pushing his prick right in.

They all moaned together -- just like it should be. Mel bucked and Brett squeezed and he pushed and yeah. Yeah, just like that. Jay moved faster, harder, pushing them all higher and higher. God, Brett was tight, squeezing down on him, and Mel's ass pushed back against him, and he thought he might just explode.

Mel reached back, fingers stroking his cheek. "Jay-love."

Kissing her fingers, he leaned harder against her back, loving her smooth skin. "Love you, honey."

"I know." Her laugh rang out, made Brett groan and squeeze around him.

"Oh. Come on you two." Brett pulled at them, pushed up against them. "I'm gonna die."

Mel snorted. "Pussy."

"Yes. More. Please?" Now it was Brett laughing,

shaking their foundation, making little earthquakes go off in his body.

Fuck, he loved them. Loved playing with them.

Mel bucked, hips pushing back hard and Brett cried out. Jamie tried hard to hold on, but he was voted most likely to blow back in their high school days and now was no better. He wrapped his arms around Mel and smacked his hips against Mel and Brett, coming hard.

He heard Brett grunt and call out, felt Mel's skin go hot and slick as she shuddered.

"Yeah. Oh. That's it." He made it until they all stopped moving before he collapsed. The he sorta slid sideways.

Mel went the other way and Brett just sprawled, touching both of them.

"This is not getting my gutters up, y'all."

Brett smacked Mel's ass. "We're having a break."

"Don't make me feed Jamie beans for a week, stud. He sleeps on your side of the bed."

Snorting, Jamie rolled a little, wrapping an arm around Mel's waist. "I sleep with whoever's warm."

She chuckled, face turned up for a kiss. "I sleep with my men."

Brett slid up between them, joining the kiss, making them all smile as their lips parted. Yeah, these days Mel slept with them. It was probably the only good thing Wayne had ever done.

It for sure was the one thing the bastard hadn't understood.

They mated for life.

Mates

Contributors

Sean Michael

Often referred to as "Space Cowboy" and "Gangsta of Love" while still striving for the moniker of "Maurice," Sean Michael spends his days surfing, smutting, organizing his immense gourd collection and fantasizing about one day retiring on a small secluded island peopled entirely by horseshoe crabs. While collecting vast amounts of vintage gay pulp novels and mood rings, Sean whiles away the hours between dropping the f-bomb and pursuing the kama sutra by channeling the long lost spirit of John Wayne and singing along with the soundtrack to "Chicago." Check out Sean's webpage at http://www.seanmichaelwrites.com/

Julia Talbot

Julia Talbot resides in the Texas and has quit her day job. She has a penchant for blank books, gay porn, and big, ugly hats. She can most often be found in coffee shops and restaurants, scribbling in her notebook and entertaining other diners with her mutterings. Julia cut her reading and writing teeth on purple-prosed romance novels, and as a result decided that boys were much more interesting with boys.

Intense study of her subject and as much firsthand research as possible figure heavily in her writing adventures. Historical and fantasy settings are Julia's favorites. Her novels include Manners and Means, Jumping Into Things, and Mysterious Ways.

BA Tortuga

BA Tortuga enjoys indulging in the shallow side of life, with hobbies that include collecting margarita recipes, hot tub dips, and ogling hot guys at the beach. A connoisseur of the perverse and esoteric, BA's days are spent among dusty tomes of ancient knowledge, or, conversely, surfing porn sites in the name of research. Mixing the natural born southern propensity for sarcasm and the environmental western straight-shooting sensibility, BA manages to produce mainstream fiction, literary erotica, and fine works of pure, unadulterated smut. Visit BA at www.batortuga.com.

Mates

Made in the USA